William Shakespeare's Macbeth: A Retelling in Prose

David Bruce

Published by David Bruce, 2022.

WILLIAM SHAKESPEARE'S MACBETH: A RETELLING IN PROSE

First edition. July 27, 2022.

Copyright © 2022 David Bruce.

ISBN: 979-8201095963

Written by David Bruce.

Table of Contents

Dedication

Dedicated to Carl Eugene Bruce and Josephine Saturday Bruce

My father, Carl Eugene Bruce, died on 24 October 2013. He used to work for Ohio Power, and at one time, his job was to shut off the electricity of people who had not paid their bills. He sometimes would find a home with an impoverished mother and some children. Instead of shutting off their electricity, he would tell the mother that she needed to pay her bill or soon her electricity would be shut off. He would write on a form that no one was home when he stopped by because if no one was home he did not have to shut off their electricity.

The best good deed that anyone ever did for my father occurred after a storm that knocked down many power lines. He and other linemen worked long hours and got wet and cold. Their feet were freezing because water got into their boots and soaked their socks. Fortunately, a kind woman gave my father and the other linemen dry socks to wear.

My mother, Josephine Saturday Bruce, died on 14 June 2003. She used to work at a store that sold clothing. One day, an impoverished mother with a baby clothed in rags walked into the store and started shoplifting in an interesting way: The mother took the rags off her baby and dressed the infant in new clothing. My mother knew that this mother could not afford to buy the clothing, but she helped the mother dress her baby and then she watched as the mother walked out of the store without paying.

***

A Buddhist monk visiting a class wrote this on the chalkboard: "EVERYONE WANTS TO SAVE THE WORLD, BUT NO ONE WANTS TO HELP MOM DO THE DISHES." The students laughed, but the monk then said, "Statistically, it's highly unlikely that any of you will ever have the opportunity to run into a burning orphanage and rescue an infant. But, in the smallest gesture of kindness — a warm smile, holding the door for the person behind you, shoveling the driveway of the elderly person next door — you have committed an act of immeasurable profundity, because to each of us, our life is our universe."

Educate Yourself
Read Like A Wolf Eats
Be Excellent to Each Other
Books Then, Books Now, Books Forever

***

In this retelling, as in all my retellings, I have tried to make the work of literature accessible to modern readers who may lack some of the knowledge about mythology, religion, and history that the literary work's contemporary audience had.

Do you know a language other than English? If you do, I give you permission to translate this book, copyright your translation, publish or self-publish it, and keep all the royalties for yourself. (Do give me credit, of course, for the original retelling.)

I would like to see my retellings of classic literature used in schools, so I give permission to the country of Finland (and all other countries) to give copies of this book to all students forever. I also give permission to the state of Texas (and all other states) to give copies of this book to all students forever. I also give permission to all teachers to give copies of this book to all students forever.

Teachers need not actually teach my retellings. Teachers are welcome to give students copies of my books as background material. For example, if they are teaching Homer's *Iliad* and *Odyssey*, teachers are welcome to give students copies of my *Virgil's* Aeneid: *A Retelling in Prose* and tell students, "Here's another ancient epic you may want to read in your spare time."

CAST OF CHARACTERS

Duncan, King of Scotland
Malcolm, Donalbain, his sons
Macbeth, Banquo, generals of the King's army
Macduff, Lennox, Ross, Menteth, Angus, Cathness, noblemen of Scotland
Fleance, son to Banquo
Siward, Earl of Northumberland, general of the English forces
Young Siward, his son
Seyton, an officer attending on Macbeth
Boy, son to Macduff
An English Doctor
A Scotch Doctor
A Captain
A Porter
An Old Man
Lady Macbeth
Lady Macduff
Gentlewomen attending on Lady Macbeth
Hecate
Three Witches
Lords, Gentlemen, Officers, Soldiers, Murderers, Attendants, and Messengers; the Ghost of Banquo, and other Apparitions

CHAPTER 1: THE TEMPTATION OF MACBETH

— 1.1 —

In a deserted place above which thunder sounded and lightning flashed, Three Witches were ending their meeting. Nearby, a battle raged, and soldiers and horses screamed and died.

"When shall we three meet again? Shall we meet in thunder and lightning, or in rain?" asked the First Witch.

"We shall meet again after the battle is over. The battle shall have its conquerors, and it shall have its conquered," answered the Second Witch.

"The battle will end before the Sun sets," said the Third Witch.

"In which place shall we meet?" asked the First Witch.

"We shall meet upon the heath," answered the Second Witch.

"There we shall meet Macbeth," said the Third Witch.

With the Witches were their familiars. Graymalkin was a malevolent spirit in the form of a gray cat, and Paddock was a malevolent spirit in the form of a toad. The familiars were growing restless.

"I come, Graymalkin!" exclaimed the First Witch.

"Paddock calls," said the Second Witch.

"It is time to go," said the Third Witch.

All together, the Three Witches chanted, "Fair is foul, and foul is fair. Hover through the fog and filthy air."

The Three Witches and their familiars vanished.

— 1.2 —

Duncan, King of Scotland, was too old to lead his soldiers in the battle, so he stood in a camp near the battle. Macbeth and Banquo were leading his soldiers. With King Duncan were his older son, Malcolm, and his younger son, Donalbain; Lennox, a nobleman; and many servants and soldiers. A soldier who was bloody from his wounds rode into the camp.

"Who is this bloody soldier?" King Duncan asked. "By the way he looks, he can provide news of how the battle is going."

2

"This good and brave soldier fought hard to keep me from being captured," Malcolm said. "Welcome, brave sergeant and friend! Tell the King news about the battle as it stood when you left it."

"In the middle of the battle, no one could tell who would win. The two sides seemed to be equal," the bloody soldier replied. "They were like two exhausted swimmers who cling to each other and prevent each other from swimming. The traitor Macdonwald — the rebel who is guilty of many evil deeds — commanded both lightly armed and heavily armed foot soldiers who had come from the Western Isles known as the Hebrides. Fortune seemed to smile at him like a whore, but brave Macbeth — and well does he deserve to be called brave — ignored Fortune, and with his sword, which steamed with hot blood, he cut his way through enemy soldiers until he faced the traitor. Macdonwald had no time to shake hands with him, or to say goodbye to him, because Macbeth immediately cut him open from his naval to his jawbone. Then he cut off the traitor's head and exhibited it to all from the top of the walls of our fortifications."

"Macbeth is both brave and worthy. He is a true gentleman," King Duncan said.

"A calm morning at sea can later turn into a stormy day that can wreck ships," the bloody soldier said. "Something that seems good can lead to something bad. Immediately after your troops had defeated the rebel and forced his troops to flee, the King of Norway sensed an opportunity to conquer Scotland and sent armed soldiers to attack your troops."

"Did not this dismay the captains of our army: Macbeth and Banquo?" King Duncan asked.

"Yes, it did," the bloody soldier replied, "exactly as much as sparrows dismay eagles, or rabbits dismay lions. Macbeth and Banquo were truly like cannons loaded with extra explosives as they fiercely fought the enemy soldiers. It was as if they wanted to bathe in the blood of the enemy soldiers, or to make the battlefield as memorable as Golgotha, where Jesus was crucified. But I am growing faint. A physician needs to treat my wounds."

"Your words and your wounds give you honor," King Duncan said to the sergeant.

Then he said to an attendant, "Get him medical help."

The attendant helped the bloody soldier walk away to a physician.

A man came into the camp, and King Duncan asked, "Who comes here?"

Malcolm recognized the man and identified him: "The worthy Thane of Ross."

A Thane is a Scottish feudal lord.

Lennox, who was also a Thane, said, "Look at his eyes! He must have important news to tell!"

"God save the King!" Ross said.

"From where have you come, worthy Thane?" King Duncan asked him.

"From Fife, great King," Ross replied. "That is the site of the battle that the King of Norway, assisted by a traitor, the Thane of Cawdor, has been fighting your troops led by Macbeth and Banquo. The Norwegian banners flew there as the King of Norway's many troops began the battle. Despite the enemy's many troops, Macbeth — wearing armor well tested in battle — fought as if he were the husband of Bellona, the goddess of war, and countered the enemy's attacks with attacks of his own and broke both the enemy's army and his spirit. Your troops have conquered the enemy and won the battle."

"This is good news indeed!" King Duncan said.

"Sweno, the King of Norway, now wants a peace treaty," Ross said. "We would not allow him to bury his dead soldiers until he gave us $10,000 and retreated to Saint Colme's island."

"The Thane of Cawdor acted as a traitor to me," King Duncan said. "That will not happen again: Proclaim that he has been sentenced to death. When you meet Macbeth, greet him and tell him that he is the new Thane of Cawdor."

"I will do so," Ross said.

"What the Thane of Cawdor has lost, noble Macbeth has won," King Duncan said.

— 1.3 —

Thunder sounded as the Three Witches met in an uncultivated field.

"Where have you been, sister?" the First Witch said.

"Killing swine — to waste food for mortals," the Second Witch replied.

The Third Witch then asked the First Witch, "Where have you been, sister?"

The First Witch replied, "A sailor's wife had chestnuts in her lap, and she munched, and munched, and munched. 'Give me your chestnuts,' I demanded. 'Get lost, witch!' the fat-bottomed, scabby sailor's wife told me. Her husband is the master of the ship *Tiger*, and he is sailing to the Syrian city Aleppo. I will sail to his ship in a kitchen strainer, and like a rat without a tail, I will wreak havoc, and wreak havoc, and wreak havoc."

"I'll give thee a wind to cause a storm," the Second Witch said.

"You are kind," the First Witch said.

"And I will give you another wind," the Third Witch said.

The First Witch said to the other Witches, "I myself have all the other winds, and I know all the ports and all the ships' shelters from all the points of the compass. I will drain away the sailor's energy. He shall not sleep, and he shall be a man accursed. For nine times nine weeks shall he decline, waste away, and long for land. Though his ship cannot be lost at sea because I lack that power, yet it shall be tempest-tossed. But, here, look what I have."

"Show me, show me," the Second Witch said.

"Here I have a pilot's thumb, whose ship was wrecked as homeward he did come," the First Witch said.

The Three Witches heard the sound of a drum.

"A drum, a drum! Macbeth does come," the Third Witch said.

The Three Witches danced in a circle and chanted, "The Weird Sisters, hand in hand, travelers of the sea and land, thus do go about, about, thrice to thine and thrice to mine, and thrice again, to make up nine. Stop! Our charm is coiled like a trap."

Macbeth and Banquo rode toward the Three Witches without at first seeing them.

"So foul and fair a day I have not seen," Macbeth said. "It is fair because we have won important battles, but foul because of the weather."

Banquo, wondering about the distance that they had left to ride to Forres, the site of King Duncan's castle, asked, "How far is it to Forres?"

Banquo then caught sight of the Three Witches and said, "Who are these creatures? They are so withered with age and wear clothing so odd that they do not seem to be creatures of the Earth, and yet here they are.

"Are you alive?" Banquo called to the Three Witches. "Are you creatures that men may talk to and ask questions of? You seem to understand me, since each of you has put a chapped finger to your skinny lips. But are you women? You seem to be women, but your beards make me question whether you are."

"Speak, if you can," Macbeth ordered. "What are you?"

The First Witch said, "All hail, Macbeth! Hail to thee, Thane of Glamis!"

The Second Witch said, "All hail, Macbeth! Hail to thee, Thane of Cawdor!"

The Third Witch said, "All hail, Macbeth, you who shall be King hereafter!"

Many men would consider it good news to become King, but Macbeth did not react as if the words of the Third Witch had made him happy.

"Sir, why do you react in such a way to news that does seem to be extraordinarily good?" Banquo said to Macbeth. "At first, you were startled, and then you seemed to be afraid."

Banquo then said to the Three Witches, "Are you illusions, or are you really what you seem to be? You have greeted Macbeth with honors that you say are real now and with the great honor that you say is coming to him. These honors of royalty and of hope to be King have made Macbeth silent as he contemplates your words. To me you have not spoken. If you are able to see into the future and can say who will prosper and who will not, tell me my future — the future of one who neither wants your love nor fears your hatred."

The First Witch said, "Hail!"

The Second Witch said, "Hail!"

The Third Witch said, "Hail!"

The First Witch said, "You are lesser than Macbeth, and greater."

The Second Witch said, "You are not so happy as Macbeth, yet much happier."

The Third Witch said, "Your descendants will be Kings, although you yourself shall never be King. So all hail, Macbeth and Banquo!"

The First Witch said, "Banquo and Macbeth, all hail!"

Macbeth said to the Three Witches, "Stay, and tell me the rest of the story. I am Thane of Glamis because my father, Sinel, died. But how can I be Thane of Cawdor? The Thane of Cawdor, a prosperous gentleman, is still alive. And to become King seems to be impossible, just like becoming Thane of Cawdor seems to be impossible. Tell me how you know these things. Tell me from where you learned these things. Tell me why you stopped Banquo and me on this heath and greeted us with prophecies. I demand that you answer my questions."

The Three Witches vanished.

"The Earth must have bubbles, just as the water has," Banquo said. "These three beings must be the bubbles of the Earth. Bubbles burst, and they vanish. Did you see where the three beings went?"

"They vanished into the air," Macbeth said. "What seemed to be solid melted away as breath melts into the wind. I wish that they had stayed!"

"Did we really see and hear what we think we saw and heard?" Banquo asked. "Or have we eaten a poisonous plant that produces insanity?"

"Your children shall be Kings," Macbeth said.

Banquo said, "You shall be King."

Wanting to hear seemingly good news again, Macbeth said, "And Thane of Cawdor, too. Isn't that what they said?"

"That is exactly what they said," Banquo replied.

Hearing a noise, Banquo said loudly, "Who is that?"

On horseback, Ross and Angus rode up to Macbeth and Banquo.

Ross said, "Macbeth, King Duncan is pleased with the news of your successes. He has heard of your personal exploits in the battle against the rebels. He is speechless with admiration at your deeds in that battle, and yet he wishes to praise you. And you did more besides. On the same day, you were fearless as you fought the soldiers from Norway. You did not fear death as you created much death for enemy soldiers. King Duncan received message after message bearing news of your bravery in battle as you defended Scotland."

Angus added, "King Duncan has sent us to you to bring you to him. He will reward you for your service."

Ross said, "King Duncan told me to inform you of one of the honors you will receive from him. You are now Thane of Cawdor. Hail, most worthy Thane!"

Amazed at hearing some of the words of the Three Witches come true, Banquo said to Macbeth, "What, can Satan speak the truth?"

Macbeth said to Ross, "The old Thane of Cawdor lives. How then can I be the new Thane of Cawdor?"

Angus answered Macbeth's question: "He who was the Thane of Cawdor still lives, but he has deservedly been sentenced to death. I don't know whether he allied himself with the King of Norway, or whether he allied himself with the rebels, or whether he allied himself with both, but I do know that he plotted against King Duncan and Scotland. I also know that the evidence of his treasons is overwhelming and that he has confessed his treasons. Thus he is sentenced to die."

Macbeth thought, *Some of the words of the Three Witches have come true. I was already Thane of Glamis, and as the Three Witches predicted, I am now Thane of Cawdor. They also predicted that I would be King of Scotland. Perhaps that also will come true.*

Macbeth said to Ross and Angus, "Thank you for this news."

Macbeth then said quietly so that only Banquo could hear him, "Do you not hope your children shall be Kings? The Three Witches who predicted that I would be the Thane of Cawdor also promised that your children shall be Kings."

Banquo quietly replied, "The Three Witches predicted that you would be King of Scotland as well as Thane of Cawdor. But I am suspicious. The forces of evil often tell us partial truths. They win us over with trifles, only to betray us in serious matters."

Banquo then said to Ross and Angus, "I need to speak to you."

As Banquo, Ross, and Angus talked among themselves, Macbeth brooded, thinking, *I now have two of the titles that the Three Witches said I would have. I have the lesser titles, and the greatest title is yet to come.*

Macbeth, realizing that he needed to add something to the conversation, said, "Gentlemen, I thank you."

Then he resumed brooding: *What the Three Witches told me cannot be ill, and it cannot be good. If what they said is ill, why has it started with a truth and with a valuable reward: the title of Thane of Cawdor? If what they said is good, why am I thinking things that make my hair stand on end and that make my heart beat unnaturally against my ribs? I felt less fear in the two battles I fought today than I do at the thoughts I am now having. I am thinking of a murder. The murder is still only imaginary, but it shakes me and I cannot perform any ordinary actions because my thoughts consume me. All I can think about is a murder.*

Banquo said to Ross and Angus, "Look at Macbeth. He is lost in his thoughts."

Macbeth continued brooding: *If I am meant to be King of Scotland, then perhaps I will become King of Scotland without having to do anything to make that happen.*

Banquo said to Ross and Angus, "He is thinking about his new honor: He is now Thane of Cawdor. After a while, he will become accustomed to that honor and wear it well, just as we become accustomed to new clothes by wearing them until they adapt to our body."

Macbeth continued brooding: *Whatever must come to pass will come to pass. I may be eager for what is to come, but if I am patient, it will eventually come.*

Banquo said, "Macbeth, we are ready to leave. Are you ready?"

"Pardon me," Macbeth said. "I was distracted by things I have already forgotten. Gentlemen, I thank you for what you have done today. I will remember you whenever I think of this day. Let us go to King Duncan."

Macbeth then said quietly to Banquo, "Think about the Three Witches, and later let us talk about them."

Banquo quietly replied, "Very gladly."

"Until later, then," Macbeth said quietly to Banquo.

Then Macbeth said loudly to all, "Let us go."

They rode on horseback to the King.

— 1.4 —

In the courtyard of King Duncan's castle in Forres, the King talked to his sons, Malcolm and Donalbain, and to Lennox. Attendants were also present.

King Duncan asked, "Has the old Thane of Cawdor been executed yet? Have his executioners returned yet?"

"My liege, they have not yet returned," Malcolm replied. "However, I have spoken with a person who saw the execution, and he reported that the old Thane of Cawdor confessed his treasons, implored that your Highness would forgive him, and repented his sins. In life, he did nothing so well as leaving it. He died as if he had studied how to die and how to throw away the dearest thing anyone can own as if it were nothing but an unwanted trifle."

King Duncan said, "It is impossible to look at a man's face and know what is in his mind. I absolutely trusted the old Thane of Cawdor."

Macbeth, Banquo, Ross, and Angus rode into the courtyard of the King's castle.

King Duncan said to Macbeth, "Worthiest kinsman, I was just now thinking that I have not shown you enough gratitude for your service to me. You have done such great service in so little time that the evidence of my gratitude is lagging behind. Only if you had done less service would I be able to give you adequate thanks and payment. You deserve more than all I have."

"Serving you and being loyal to you are rewards in and of themselves," Macbeth replied. "As our King, you should receive our service to you. We — your subjects — are your children and your servants. By doing everything we can to safeguard your love and your honor, we are doing only what we ought to do."

King Duncan said to Macbeth, "I will do much for you. I have begun to plant you, and I will work to make you full of growing."

He added, "Noble Banquo, like Macbeth you deserve reward for your deeds. I will hold you in my heart. I also will do good things for you."

Banquo replied, "If you make me grow, I shall give you the harvest."

"I have so many joys that my eyes are watery," King Duncan said. "Sons, kinsmen, Thanes, and all of you who are closest to me, know that I am establishing the succession of the kingdom upon my oldest son, Malcolm, whom I name Prince of Cumberland. This is an honor for him, and more honors will be given to all who deserve them. Now let us go to Macbeth's castle in Inverness."

King Duncan said to Macbeth, "I will become bound to you even further because I will enjoy your hospitality."

Macbeth replied, "When I am not working to serve you, leisure is labor. I will tell my wife the news of your coming to our castle and so make her happy. Therefore, I humbly take my leave."

King Duncan replied, "Farewell, my worthy Thane of Cawdor."

As he left, Macbeth thought, *Malcolm is now Prince of Cumberland! He is now the heir to the throne! I must give up my ambition or else leap over Malcolm because he stands between me and my desire to become King. Stars, hide your fires; I do not want light to see my black and deep desires. May my eye not see what my hand will do; still, let the deed occur that the eye will fear to see when the deed is done.*

After Macbeth left, King Duncan and Banquo talked to each other and praised Macbeth. Now King Duncan said, "You are correct, Banquo. Macbeth is very valiant, and I enjoy hearing him praised. Your praises of him are like a banquet to me. Let us leave and ride to his castle, where he has gone to prepare our welcome. He is a peerless kinsman."

In a room in Macbeth's castle in Inverness, Lady Macbeth was reading a letter that Macbeth had sent to her.

She read out loud, "The Three Witches met me after my successes in battle, and I have learned that they have more than merely mortal knowledge. I wanted to question them further, but they turned themselves into air and vanished. As I stood astonished, the King's messengers arrived and said that I am the new Thane of Cawdor — which is one of the titles the Weird Sisters had hailed me by. They also referred to a title to come when they said to me, 'All hail, Macbeth, you who shall be King hereafter!' I wrote this letter to you, dear, so that you may be gladdened by the prediction, and not lose happiness through ignorance of your own future title: Queen. Keep this prediction secret. Farewell."

Having finished reading the letter, Lady Macbeth thought, *You are the Thane of Glamis, and you are the Thane of Cawdor, and you will be the King of Scotland. Yet I am afraid that you do not have in you to do what it will take to make you King. Your nature is too full of the milk of human kindness to do what will most quickly make you King. You, Macbeth, would like to be a great and powerful man. You have ambition, but you lack the evil nature that so often accompanies and assists ambition. What you most want, you would like to have through honest means. You do not want to do evil, and yet you want something that belongs to someone else. Macbeth, what you need to have is a nature that tells you, "This is what you need to do to achieve your ambition." You also need a nature that allows you to do an evil act that you fear to do rather than a nature that wishes an evil act to remain undone. Come quickly to me, so that I can talk to you and persuade you to ignore the part of your nature that can keep you from wearing the crown of the King of Scotland. Both fate and supernatural beings seem to know that you will be King.*

A messenger entered the room Lady Macbeth was in.

Lady Macbeth asked, "What news do you bring me?"

The messenger replied, "The King comes here tonight."

Lady Macbeth said, "You must be insane! Isn't Macbeth with the King? If what you said is true, Macbeth would have sent me word to prepare the castle for the King's arrival."

The messenger replied, "So please you, it is true. Macbeth is coming here. Another messenger traveled faster than Macbeth to bring you news. That messenger was so out of breath that he scarcely had enough to speak his news."

"Take care of him," Lady Macbeth said. "He has brought us important news."

The messenger left.

Lady Macbeth thought, *The messenger is like a hoarse raven as he announces the fatal entrance of King Duncan into my castle.*

She then prayed silently to unHeavenly spirits: *Come, you spirits that tend on deadly thoughts. Unsex me, and make me not a woman. Fill me from top to bottom with the worst kind of cruelty. Make my blood thick, and stop my monthly periods. Make me incapable of feeling remorse. Make me a man so that nothing feminine can stop me from accomplishing the evil I plan to do. Come to my woman's breasts, and replace my milk with gall, you murdering spirits. Come to me from wherever you, invisible, assist in the doing of evil. Come, thick night, and enshroud yourself in the darkest smoke of Hell, so that no one can see the wound my keen knife makes and so that Heaven cannot see through the darkness and shout, "Stop! Stop!"*

Macbeth entered the room.

Lady Macbeth said to him, "Great Glamis! Worthy Cawdor! You will have a title greater than both of these. I have read your letter, and it has taken me beyond this present time, which normally does not know the future. Now I know the future."

Macbeth said, "My dearest love, King Duncan comes here tonight."

"And when does he leave?" Lady Macbeth asked.

"He intends to leave tomorrow," Macbeth replied.

"Never shall Sun rise on the day that King Duncan leaves here alive," Lady Macbeth said. "Your face, Macbeth, is at present like a book on which people can read your thoughts, including your evil thoughts. To fool the people around you, look like the people around you. Your eye should welcome the King. Your hands and your tongue should welcome the King. You should look like an innocent flower, but in reality you must be the serpent under it. We must take care of the King, and I want you to let me plan how to take care of the King. What we do this night will give us during all the nights and days to come absolute power."

Macbeth said, "We will speak further about this."

Lady Macbeth said, "In public, look innocent. If you look anything but innocent, we have much to fear. Leave all the rest to me."

— 1.6 —

King Duncan, Malcolm, Donalbain, Banquo, Lennox, Macduff, Ross, Angus, and some attendants entered the courtyard of Macbeth's castle.

Looking around, King Duncan said, "This castle has a pleasant site; the air immediately and sweetly soothes my senses."

Banquo said, "The guests of summer — the birds known as the martlets that are often seen around temples — provide evidence for what you say because their hanging nests are everywhere here. Every jetty, every frieze, and every corner has its nest. Where the martlets build nests and live, there I have observed that the air is delicate."

Lady Macbeth came outside to the courtyard to greet the group.

"See, see, our honorable hostess," King Duncan said. "Sometimes, people who love me inconvenience me with their attention, but I accept it because of the love they have for me. I hope that you will give me the same courtesy. By coming to your castle, I am inconveniencing you, but I have come here because of the love I have for you and your husband. I often ask God to give rewards to the people who inconvenience me, and I thank them for their attentions to me. Perhaps by my visit I can teach you to do the same for me."

Lady Macbeth replied, "All the service we provide for you is poor and trivial even if it were done twice and then done twice more. All the service we provide for you does not come even close to matching the honor you do us by coming to our castle. Because of the honors you have given to us in the past, and because of the new honors you have recently given to us, we are your hermits and pray to God to bless you, our benefactor."

"Where is the Thane of Cawdor?" King Duncan asked. "We rode close behind him — almost at his heels — and we even thought of arriving here before him to make preparations for his arrival, but he rode his horse well, and his great love for his King and for his country — a love as sharp as the spurs he wears — helped him to reach his castle before we did. Fair and noble hostess, I am your guest tonight."

"We are your servants," Lady Macbeth replied, "and all we have, including our lives, we have in trust from you. We are always ready to give an accounting of all we have, and we are always ready to give back to you what is yours."

"Give me your hand," King Duncan said, "Take me to my host. I love him highly, and I shall continue to show favor to him. Are you ready, hostess?"

Lady Macbeth led King Duncan and the other guests inside the castle.

— 1.7 —

Inside Macbeth's castle, servants prepared a feast for King Duncan.

Macbeth, alone, thought to himself, *If it were over and done once it were done, then it would be good to do it quickly. If only I could assassinate King Duncan, and then like a net catch all the consequences that follow except for my becoming King of Scotland ... if this one blow — the assassination — by itself could make me King of Scotland with no bad consequences following in this life ... if that were the case, then in order to be King of Scotland now I would risk damnation in the life hereafter. But would no consequences follow? In this life and in this world, we have laws and courts and executions. Also, by committing bloody acts, we teach other people to commit bloody acts, and we can end up being the victim and not the victimizer in the next bloody act. Or we can end up being harmed in other ways. If we poison wine to offer to other people, sometimes that poisoned wine is justly offered to ourselves.*

What reasons do I have to murder King Duncan? What reasons do I have to not murder him? King Duncan is my kinsman, and I am his subject. These are reasons not to kill King Duncan. In addition, I am his host. As his host, I ought to protect him against murderers, not carry a knife with which to murder him. Also, as King of Scotland, Duncan has been a good King. He has great power, but he has used his power fairly and justly. He has been free of vice. His virtues plead against his murder. Should he be murdered, pity would spread quickly to his subjects as if the news of the murder were carried by a newborn babe riding the wind, or like winged angels riding on the winds of the Earth — the tears of King Duncan's sorrowing subjects will fall like rain and drown the wind. I have no good reason to murder King Duncan. I have only my ambition to be King of Scotland. This ambition can vault over good reasons not to do something. This vaulting ambition is like a rider who tries to leap into a saddle but overleaps and falls to the ground on the other side of the horse.

Seeing his wife enter the room, Macbeth asked, "What is the news?"

Lady Macbeth replied, "King Duncan has almost finished eating. Why did you leave the dining chamber?"

Macbeth asked, "Has King Duncan asked for me?"

"Of course he has," Lady Macbeth replied.

"We will proceed no further in this business we have been planning," Macbeth said. "King Duncan has greatly honored me recently. I have earned golden opinions from all sorts of people. Because they are new, I should enjoy these golden opinions for a while, not throw them away as if they were old clothes."

Lady Macbeth replied, "You were hopeful of quickly becoming King. Was your hope drunk? Did your hope sleep off its drunkenness? Has your hope woken up with a hangover? Does it now look sickly and pale at what it wanted to acquire? From this time on, I know how to value your love. You know what you want. Are you afraid to act to get it? Will you act to get the crown you desire, or will you live like a coward and know that you are a coward? Will you allow 'I will get what I want' to always be followed by 'I dare not act to get what I want'? Will you be like the cat in this old proverb: 'The cat wants to eat fish, but it will not wet its feet'?"

"Please shut up," Macbeth said. "I dare do all that a man may do. Who dares do more than I do is not a man."

"When you brought up the idea of murdering King Duncan to me, were you then a beast?" Lady Macbeth asked. "No. When you dared to murder King Duncan, then you were a man. And if you actually commit the murder, then you will be even more of a man. Before, the proper time and place of the murder was not known, and you dared to think of murder. Now, the time and place — this night, here in our castle — are known. Before, you thought to make a proper time and place for murder, but now that you have them, you are afraid to commit murder. I have breastfed an infant, and I know how it is to love the babe who feeds at my breast, but I would, while the babe was smiling in my sight, have plucked my nipple from his boneless gums, and dashed his brains out, had I sworn as you have sworn to commit murder."

Macbeth asked, "What happens if we are caught?"

Lady Macbeth replied, "Why should we be caught? Call up your courage, and we will not be caught. When King Duncan is asleep — and after this day's hard journey he will soon be asleep — I will get his two bodyguards drunk with wine. They will remember nothing, and their brains will be confused with alcohol and the drugs I will put in their wine. When they are asleep like drunken pigs, what cannot you and I do to the unguarded King Duncan? What can we do that we cannot put the blame upon his drunken bodyguards? They shall bear the blame of our great murder."

Macbeth said, "Give birth to sons only, not to daughters, for your undaunted spirit should bring forth only sons. After we kill King Duncan, we can smear his blood on his bodyguards and on their daggers. Will that be enough to make other people think that King Duncan's bodyguards have murdered him?"

Lady Macbeth replied, "What else will anyone be able to think? After all, you and I shall loudly grieve for the murdered King."

Macbeth said, "I have made up my mind. I shall force every part of my body to do the terrible deed I have decided to do. Let us rejoin the feast and fool the others with our acting skills. False faces must hide what the false heart does know."

CHAPTER 2: MACBETH TURNS EVIL

— 2.1 —

In the darkness of night, Banquo and Fleance, his son, entered the courtyard of Macbeth's castle. To provide light, Fleance carried a burning torch.

Banquo asked, "Fleance, what time of night is it?"

Fleance replied, "The Moon has set. I have not heard the clock."

"I believe that the Moon sets at twelve."

"I am sure that it is later than that."

Banquo said, "Hold my sword for me."

He thought, *We are in Macbeth's castle, and we ought to fear nothing while we are here. I should have no need to carry a sword.*

He said out loud, "The Heavens tonight are practicing frugality. The candles that are the stars are not burning. I do not wish to carry anything tonight. I am so tired that I ought to go to bed, and yet, I do not want to sleep. I pray that God and the saints will keep from me the nightmares that come while men sleep."

Macbeth and a servant made a slight noise as they entered the courtyard.

Startled by the noise, Banquo ordered Fleance, "Give me my sword!" Then he called out, "Who's there?"

Macbeth replied, "A friend."

Banquo said, "I am surprised that you are not yet in bed. The King is at his rest. He is very pleased with your hospitality and with your recent heroism, and he has given to you and your lady many gifts. Here is a diamond that he gave to me to give to you as a present for Lady Macbeth in gratitude for the hospitality he has received here. He called her 'a most kind hostess,' and when he went to bed he was most content with your reception of him here."

Macbeth replied, "We were unprepared for King Duncan's visit to our castle, and so although we greatly desired to entertain him well, we were unable to do all that we had wished."

"All is well," Banquo said, and then he changed the subject. "I dreamed last night of the three Weird Sisters. Some of what they said about you has proved to be true. You are now the Thane of Cawdor."

17

"I have not been thinking about them," Macbeth lied, and then he added, "And yet, if sometime you and I can spare an hour, we could meet and talk about the Weird Sisters, if you are willing."

"I will be happy to do so whenever you like," Banquo said.

"Sometime in the future, I will desire your support," Macbeth said. "If you give me that support, you will benefit by so doing."

"I will be happy to support your cause, as long as I do not lose honor by so doing," Banquo said. Thinking of the Weird Sisters' prophecy that Macbeth would in the future be King of Scotland, Banquo added, "I would hate to lose the honor I already have by attempting to gain more honor. I will be happy to support your cause as long as I can keep my conscience clean and my loyalty to King Duncan unspotted."

"Sleep well," Macbeth said.

"Thank you, sir," Banquo said. "You do the same."

Banquo and Fleance left the courtyard, leaving Macbeth and the servant behind.

Macbeth ordered the servant, "Go to Lady Macbeth. Tell her that when she has finished mixing my drink to ring a bell. Then go to bed."

The servant left, leaving Macbeth alone.

Macbeth then saw something that nobody else, if anyone had been present, would have seen.

Macbeth thought, *Is this a dagger that I see before me, the handle toward my hand? Come, let me clutch it.*

He made a motion to grab the dagger, but his hand closed on nothing.

I do not have it in my hand, and yet I see it clearly. Is this fatal vision unable to be touched as well as to be seen? Is this dagger simply a creation of my mind? Is it a hallucination produced by my fevered brain? I see the dagger, and it appears to be as solid as the dagger that now I draw.

Macbeth drew a dagger from his belt.

The dagger I cannot touch leads me in the direction that I must go to kill the King. The dagger I cannot touch is like the dagger that I will use to kill the King. My eyes are not working correctly although my other senses do work, or perhaps my eyes work even better than my other senses. I see the dagger clearly. On it I now see splashes of blood that were not on it previously.

No bloody knife is here. My thinking of murdering King Duncan has caused me to hallucinate this knife. Half of the world is now asleep and lying as if they were dead, and nightmares prey upon them in their beds that are curtained in an attempt to keep out the cold. Now is the time that witches give offerings to their goddess: Hecate with her dark and unsavory ways. Now is the time that the old man who is Murder, called to action by his guard the wolf, walks like Tarquin, the son of the Roman king Lucius Tarquinius Superbus, walked to rape Lucretia and cause her to commit suicide. Old man Murder walks like a ghost. Earth upon which I walk, I pray to you that you do not hear my steps. The stones I walk on ought not to reveal my presence with noise. The deed that I will do requires silence. I am thinking now, and as long as I keep thinking, King Duncan remains alive. The more I think, the more afraid I am.

A bell rang.

I go now to do the deed. The bell is my signal. Hear not the bell, King Duncan, for it is a knell that summons you to Heaven or to Hell.

Macbeth walked toward the King's bedchamber.

— 2.2 —

Lady Macbeth nervously paced and thought, *I gave the King's bodyguards wine to make them drunk; the same wine has made me bold. The wine that has put them to sleep has excited me and made me wide awake.*

A cry sounded in the night.

What was that! It was an owl, hooting while flying over a house in which a man will die. This owl is like a bellman whose job is to ring a bell to announce that a person is dying.

Macbeth is now committing the murder. I have unlocked the doors to the King's bedchamber, and the King's bodyguards are snoring, not protecting the King. Their performance of their job is laughable. I drugged their drinks so much that the bodyguards are poisoned — even if Macbeth does nothing to them, they have as much chance of dying as they do of living.

She heard Macbeth's voice calling from inside the castle, "Who's there? What's wrong?"

Lady Macbeth thought, *I am afraid that the bodyguards have woken up and stopped the murder. My husband and I will be ruined by what we have attempted and not by what we have done. Let me listen carefully. We may yet succeed. I put the daggers where my husband could not miss them. Had King Duncan not resembled my father as he slept, I would have killed him myself.*

Macbeth walked toward Lady Macbeth, who exclaimed, "My husband!"

Macbeth said, "I have done the deed. Did you hear a noise?"

Lady Macbeth replied, "I heard the owl scream and the crickets cry. Did not you speak?"

"When?"

"Just now."

"As I descended from the King's bedchamber?"

"Yes."

Macbeth, hearing an imaginary noise, said, "Listen!" Then he asked, "Who is sleeping in the bedchamber next to the King's?"

"Donalbain, King Duncan's younger son."

Macbeth looked down at his bloody hands and said, "This is a sorry sight."

Lady Macbeth replied, "A foolish thought, to say a sorry sight."

"As I descended from the King's bedchamber, I heard two people. One laughed in his sleep, and the other cried, 'Murder!' The two woke each other. I stood quietly and listened. They said their prayers and then went back to sleep."

"Two people are sleeping in that bedchamber: Donalbain and his attendant," Lady Macbeth said.

Macbeth said, "One cried, 'God bless us!' and the other cried, 'Amen.' It was as if they had seen me with these hands that look as if they belong to a hangman, bloody from chopping up the bodies of criminals after a public hanging. I listened to the two men's fears, and I could not say 'Amen' when they cried, 'God bless us!'"

"Don't think about it," Lady Macbeth said.

Macbeth asked, "But why couldn't I say 'Amen'? I had most need of blessing, and the word 'Amen' stuck in my throat."

Lady Macbeth replied, "We must not think about our evil deeds in such a fashion. Thinking about them in that way will make us mad."

"I heard a voice cry, 'Sleep no more! Macbeth does murder sleep' — the innocent sleep, sleep that relieves the cares of life, sleep that ends the hard work of the day, sleep that bathes away the soreness of hard work, sleep that heals hurt minds, sleep that most substantially nourishes the body and the mind —"

"What do you mean? I can't understand what you are saying!"

Macbeth said, "The voice cried, 'Sleep no more!' to everyone in the castle. It cried, 'Glamis has murdered sleep, and therefore Cawdor shall sleep no more. Macbeth shall sleep no more.'"

Lady Macbeth asked, "Who was it that thus cried? Husband, you weaken yourself when you think in such a cowardly way. Go. Get some water so that you can wash away the blood from your hands."

She looked at his hands and was startled by what she saw: "Why did you bring these daggers from the murder scene? They must lie there. They are evidence that will convict the King's bodyguards of murder and treason. Carry them back and smear the sleepy bodyguards with blood."

Macbeth replied, "I will not go back. I am afraid to think what I have done. Look on it again I dare not."

Lady Macbeth exclaimed, "Coward! Give me the daggers! Sleeping people and dead people are as harmless as pictures. Only a child is afraid of a picture of a devil. If King Duncan still bleeds, I will paint the faces of the bodyguards with blood. The gilding I do to their faces will result in everyone assuming that they are guilty."

She left.

A knocking sounded at the castle gate.

Macbeth thought, *Who is knocking? What is wrong with me? Every noise I hear scares me.*

He looked at his hands and said to himself, "What kind of hands are these? They seem to pluck out my eyes. Will all the water in Neptune's ocean wash away this blood from my hands? No! Instead, the blood from my hands will turn the ocean red."

Lady Macbeth overheard Macbeth's final words as she returned. She said, "My hands are now the same color — red — as your hands, but I would be ashamed if my heart were as white — as cowardly — as your heart."

A knocking sounded again at the castle gate.

She said, "I hear a knocking at the south entry. Let us go to our bedchamber. We can wash the blood from our hands and so remove the evidence that would convict us: A little water clears us of this deed, making it easy to escape punishment. You would know this, if you could keep your firmness of purpose."

More knocking sounded at the castle gate.

Lady Macbeth said, "Listen! More knocking! Let's go to our bedchamber so you can put on your dressing gown and robe. We can't be seen in these, our day clothes. People will know that we have been up and about, not sleeping. Pay attention! You are lost in your thoughts!"

Macbeth replied, "To know my deed, it were best not know myself — I had rather not know myself than to realize the full enormity of what I have done."

More knocking sounded at the castle gate.

He added, "Wake Duncan with your knocking! I wish you could!"

The Macbeths went to their bedchamber.

— 2.3 —

More knocking sounded as a half-asleep, half-drunken gatekeeper came to open the gate.

The gatekeeper complained aloud to himself, "Here's a knocking indeed! If a man were the keeper of Hell-gate, he would be kept busy turning the key."

More knocking.

"I am kept so busy that I might as well be Hell's gatekeeper, and this castle might as well be Hell. So be it. Who's there, in the name of Beelzebub, Prince of demons? Ah, here is the first knocker: A farmer who hoarded crops in the expectation of making a killing with high prices when a famine arrived. The famine never came; instead, crops were plentiful, and the farmer hanged himself because of low prices for his crops. I hope that he brought plenty of handkerchiefs with him because here in Hell he will sweat."

More knocking sounded.

"Who's there, in another devil's name that I cannot remember? It is probably a liar who told one lie that resulted in treason and when caught he told another lie: He said that the first lie did not count because he had lied for the sake of God. This liar was talented, but he was not talented enough to lie his way into Heaven, and so he knocks at Hell's gate, where he is welcomed in — and tortured."

More knocking sounded.

"Knock, knock, knock! Who's there? By my faith, here's an English tailor. For years, he stole cloth from his customers by making the garments close fitting. But he tried that trick with French stockings, which are already close fitting, and so his thievery was discovered. I hope that the tailor brought a goose with him because surely his goose will be cooked here."

22

More knocking sounded.

"Knock, knock, knock! Never any silence. But I will cease to be the gatekeeper of Hell — this place is too cold for Hell! But if I had been the gatekeeper of Hell just now, I would have let in a few more workers of different jobs who travel a broad and seemingly pleasant path to everlasting fire and torment."

More knocking sounded.

"I'm coming! I'm coming!"

The gatekeeper opened the gate and said, "Don't forget to tip."

Macduff and Lennox, two Scottish noblemen, entered the courtyard.

Macduff said to the gatekeeper, "Was it so late, friend, before you went to bed, that you lay asleep so long?"

The gatekeeper replied, "Truly, sir, we were drinking and partying until about 3 a.m., and drinking, sir, is a great provoker of three things."

"What three things does drink especially provoke?"

"Nose-painting, sleep, and urine. Much use of alcohol paints one's nose red, it makes one sleep, and it makes one pee. Alcohol both provokes and unprovokes lechery. It makes a man feel horny, and it makes a man unable to produce a horn. When it comes to horniness, alcohol is a liar. Alcohol makes a man horny, but it makes him unable to do anything about it. Alcohol persuades a man to find a partner, but it makes him unable to do anything with that partner. Alcohol makes a man attempt to get an erection, but it makes the man unable to keep that erection if he gets one. In short, alcohol lies to a man, making him horny but unable to do anything but sleep. Furthermore, once the man is asleep, the alcohol leaves him — the man pees himself."

Macduff said, "I believe that alcohol did these things to you last night."

"Alcohol did indeed, sir. It got me right in the throat. But I fought him. It made my legs weak and staggery, but I was too strong and cast it out of my body with my vomit."

Macduff asked, "Is your master awake?"

Macbeth entered the courtyard.

Seeing him, Macduff said, "Our knocking has awakened him; here he comes."

Lennox greeted Macbeth, "Good morning, noble sir."

"Good morning to both of you," Macbeth replied.

"Is the King stirring, worthy Thane?" asked Macduff.

"Not yet."

"He did command me to call early on him. I am almost too late."

"I'll bring you to him," Macbeth said.

"I know that entertaining the King is a trouble to you, but one that you are happy to undertake."

"Work that we delight in is not work," Macbeth replied. He added, "This is the door."

"I'll be so bold to wake him, as that is my appointed duty."

Macduff walked through the door that led to the King's bedchamber.

Lennox asked, "Is the King leaving here today?"

"Yes," Macbeth said. "He did decide so."

"The night has been wild," Lennox said. "Last night, the chimneys were blown down in the place we slept. People are saying that they heard cries of mourning in the air, strange screams of death, and terrible voices making prophecies of dire tumult and chaotic events to come and make the world woeful. The bird of darkness, the owl, screamed all night. Some say that the Earth was fevered and did shake."

Macbeth replied, "It was a rough night."

For Macbeth, especially, it was.

"I am too young to remember a night as bad as this," Lennox said.

Macduff ran into the courtyard and shouted, "Raise the alarm! Something has happened that is beyond words and beyond belief!"

Macbeth and Lennox asked together, "What's the matter?"

Macduff shouted, "Evil has created a masterpiece! The King's body was a temple, but the temple has been broken into and the life inside stolen!"

"What are you saying?" Macbeth asked. "The life?"

"Are you saying that King Duncan is dead?" Lennox asked.

"Go into the King's bedchamber, and you will see a sight that is like a Gorgon that will make you blind and turn you into stone," Macduff answered. "This sight will destroy anyone who sees it. I can't speak of it. Go and see it, and speak for me."

Macbeth and Lennox went through the door that led to the King's bedchamber.

Macduff shouted, "Awake, awake, everyone! Ring the alarm bell. Murder and treason! Banquo and Donalbain! Malcolm! Wake up! Shake off your sleep, which resembles death, and see real death itself! Get up! See an image of the Last Judgment! Malcolm! Banquo! Rise from your beds as if you were rising from your graves, and walk like ghosts to come and see this horror! Ring the bell!"

The alarm bell rang.

Lady Macbeth entered the courtyard and said, "What's the matter? Why has the alarm sounded to wake up everyone in the castle? It sounds like a trumpet in time of war! Tell me!"

"Gentle lady," Macduff said, "it is not for you to hear what I can speak. Such words entering a woman's ear would kill the hearer."

Banquo arrived, and Macduff said to him, "Banquo, Banquo, our royal master is murdered!"

Lady Macbeth exclaimed, "What, in our castle!"

Banquo pointed out, "Too cruel anywhere," and then he said, "Dear Macduff, I pray that you contradict yourself, and say that what you said is not so."

Macbeth, Lennox, and Ross entered the courtyard.

Macbeth said, "Had I but died an hour before this murder, I would have lived a blessed life."

Macbeth's words were true.

He added, "From this moment, there is nothing worthwhile in mortal life. Everything is a sick joke; renown and grace are dead. The wine of life has been drunk, and all that is left are the dregs."

For Macbeth, his words were true.

Malcolm and Donalbain, King Duncan's two sons, entered the courtyard.

"What's wrong?" Donalbain asked.

"You have suffered a tragedy and do not yet know it," Macbeth answered. "The spring, the head, the fountain of your blood has been stopped."

"Your royal father has been murdered," Macduff said in plain language.

"By whom?" asked Malcolm, the oldest son.

"It seems that his bodyguards committed the murder," Lennox replied. "Their hands and faces were bloodied; so were their unwiped daggers, which we found lying on their pillows. The bodyguards were disoriented and not in possession of their senses. No man's life should be trusted with them."

"I am sorry that I killed them in my fury," Macbeth said.

"Why did you kill them?" Macduff asked.

"Who can be wise and amazed, temperate and furious, loyal and neutral, all in the same moment? No one. My love for King Duncan was stronger than my reason. I saw King Duncan dead. His silver skin was laced with his golden blood. The gashes that the knives made in his body were intrusions of evil. Near the King were his murderers, red with the color of their trade, their daggers bloody with gore. In that moment, what man who loves the King could refrain from killing the King's murderers?"

Realizing that Macduff suspected her husband, Lady Macbeth created a distraction. She shouted, "Help me hence!"

Macduff ordered, "Look after the lady."

Lady Macbeth pretended to faint.

Malcolm and Donalbain, who were at a distance from the others, conferred together. No one overheard them.

Malcolm asked Donalbain, "Why are we quiet? It is our father who has been murdered."

Donalbain replied, "Why should we speak — or even be present? Our father the King is dead; those who wanted him dead will want us dead as well. I don't believe that our father's murderer or murderers have been killed. Let us flee — our lives are in danger. We can mourn our father's death later — from a safe distance. If we stay here, we can be killed at any time."

Malcolm said, "It is not yet the time to mourn — or to take action."

Banquo said, "Look after the lady."

Attendants came and carried Lady Macbeth away from the courtyard.

Banquo said, "Let us get out of our night clothing and put on warm clothing for the day, then let us meet and discuss this murder. Right now, we are shaken by our fears and suspicions. I will put my trust in God, and I will seek to find the reasons for this murder. I will fight whatever lies led to the secret plot that resulted in this murder."

"So will I," Macduff said.

"So will we all," the others said.

"Let us quickly get dressed and arm ourselves and meet in the hall," Macbeth said.

All left the courtyard except Malcolm and Donalbain.

Malcolm asked Donalbain, "What will you do? Let us not meet with them. I think the murderer is still alive and in the castle. I also think that anyone who is capable of committing a murder is also capable of pretending to be shocked and surprised at that murder. I will flee to England."

Donalbain replied, "I will flee to Ireland. If we flee in different directions, both of us will be safer than if we flee together. If we stay here, a man who smiles at us may also hide a dagger that he hopes to use to kill us. Anyone who wants to be King knows that he must kill us. Men who are the closest to us in being blood relatives are also the likeliest to make us bloody."

Malcolm said, "This treasonous plot has not yet run its course. It is as if an arrow is aimed at us. The best way for us not to be hit by the arrow is to get beyond the distance that it can travel. Therefore, let us get horses, and let us not be squeamish about leaving immediately. Let us steal ourselves away. There is no criminality in such a theft when we will meet with no mercy if we stay here."

They left the courtyard.

— 2.4 —

Outside Macbeth's castle, Ross and an old man talked.

The old man said, "I can remember well seventy years. During those years I have seen dreadful hours and strange things, but what I have seen this dark night makes those hours and things seem like trifles."

"Old man," Ross said, "the Heavens seem to be troubled by the actions of Humankind and so threaten the world in which men live. Look at a clock, and you will know that it should be daylight now, yet night strangles the Sun. Is the night too strong, or is the day too ashamed, that the result is that darkness makes the Earth dark like a tomb at a time when sunshine should enlighten it?"

"This darkness is unnatural," the old man said, "like the regicide that just occurred. Last Tuesday, an owl that normally kills mice instead attacked and killed a falcon — a bird of prey."

Ross replied, "King Duncan's horses did something that is strange. Beauteous and swift, the best of their race, these horses turned wild in nature, broke out of their stalls, and ran away. They refused to be obedient to their human masters, but instead seemed to war against them."

The old man said, "It is said that the horses cannibalized each other."

"They did," Ross said. "I myself witnessed them eating each other's flesh."

He looked to the side and said, "Here comes a good man: Macduff."

Ross said to Macduff, "How goes the world, sir, now?"

"Don't you know?" Macduff replied.

"Is it known who did this bloody, terrible regicide?"

"The bodyguards whom Macbeth has slain."

"Such evil is difficult to believe," Ross said. "In what way would the bodyguards benefit by King Duncan's murder?"

"They were paid to commit the murder. Malcolm and Donalbain, the King's two sons, have fled, and so they are being blamed for bribing the bodyguards to kill their father the King."

"Patricide and regicide! Patricide is even more against nature than regicide! Ambition can be so strong that it causes the destruction of everything in its path, including one's own father. Most likely, I suppose, Macbeth will become King. He is a close kinsman of the late King."

"He has already been chosen King, and he has gone to Scone, where he will be crowned."

"Where is the body of King Duncan?"

"It has been carried to Colmekill, where is the tomb that protects the bones of his ancestors."

"Will you go to Scone?" Ross asked.

"No, I will return to Fife, my home," Macduff replied.

Ross thought, *Macbeth could take your absence as an insult to him.* He said aloud, "I will go to Scone to see Macbeth crowned."

"I hope that all goes well there. Let me say farewell to you now. The old King was generous and merciful, and things may not go nearly as well under the new King."

Ross said, "Farewell, old man."

The old man replied, "Farewell, and may God's blessing go with you, and with all who try to turn bad things into good things and evil people into good people."

CHAPTER 3: EVIL AND MORE EVIL

— 3.1 —

Banquo stood alone at King Duncan's castle, now occupied by the Macbeths, in Forres.

Banquo thought, *Macbeth, you have it all now. You are King of Scotland and now use the royal plural. You are also Thane of Cawdor and Thane of Glamis. You have everything that the Weird Sisters promised to you, and I fear that you have acted most foully to get everything that they promised to you. However, the Weird Sisters did not say that your descendants would be Kings. Instead, they said that I would be the root and ancestor of many Kings. Since the Weird Sisters have spoken the truth to you, Macbeth, why may not they have spoken the truth to me? But I had better be quiet and not talk about this.*

A trumpet call sounded to announce the King, and King Macbeth, Queen Macbeth, Lennox, Ross, and various lords and attendants entered the room in which Banquo stood.

Macbeth said, "Here is our chief guest for tonight's banquet."

"If Banquo were not at our feast," Lady Macbeth said, "then it would be incomplete and unfitting."

"Tonight we will hold a ceremonious feast, and I request that you attend," Macbeth said to Banquo.

"It is my duty to do whatever you command," Banquo replied.

"Will you ride on horseback this afternoon?" Macbeth asked Banquo.

"Yes, my good lord."

"We would otherwise have sought your advice, which has always been serious and profitable, in today's council; however, we will hear your advice tomorrow. Will you be riding far?"

"I will ride long enough to fill the time between now and the feast. Unless my horse is faster than I expect, it will be dark for an hour or two before I return."

Macbeth ordered, "Fail not to attend our feast."

"My lord, I will not," Banquo promised.

"We hear that our blood-covered cousins — Malcolm and Donalbain — are in England and in Ireland. They deny that they cruelly murdered their father, King Duncan. Instead, they are telling their hosts strange lies. But we will talk of this tomorrow, as well as of other matters that concern us both. Go and mount your horse. Farewell, until you return. Is Fleance, your son, riding with you?"

"Yes, my good lord," Banquo replied. "And we ought to be going now."

"I hope that your horses are swift and sure of foot, and now I entrust you to their backs. Farewell."

Banquo departed, and Macbeth said to the others present, "Let everyone entertain himself until seven this evening, the time of the feast. To make company more enjoyable, we will stay by ourselves until the time of the banquet. Until then, God be with you."

All departed except for Macbeth and an attendant.

Macbeth said to the attendant, "Are the men I am expecting waiting for me?"

The attendant replied, "Yes, they are, my lord. They are outside the castle gate."

"Bring them to me."

The attendant departed, and Macbeth thought, *To be King is nothing unless I can be King without worrying about being deposed. I am deeply afraid of Banquo. His royal nature must be feared because of his many good qualities. He is courageous, and he is wise enough to tip the odds in his favor and then take action. I am afraid of no one but him. Even my guardian spirit is afraid of him, just as Mark Antony's guardian spirit was afraid of Octavian Caesar, who eventually defeated him in Rome's civil wars. Banquo rebuked the Weird Sisters when they said that I would be King, and he asked them to tell his future. They said that he would beget many Kings. To me they gave a fruitless crown and a barren scepter — according to the Weird Sisters, no son of mine will become King after me. I have defiled my mind. Why? For Banquo's descendants! I have murdered the gracious King Duncan. Why? For Banquo's descendants! I have put poisonous drugs into the cup — my conscience — from which I formerly drank only peace. Why? For Banquo's descendants! I have given my immortal soul to Satan. Why? For Banquo's descendants! I have done all these things so that Banquo's descendants may become Kings. I don't want that to happen, so I will challenge fate itself and fight it to the death.*

Hearing a noise, Macbeth asked, "Who's there?"

The attendant came again into the room, bringing with him two murderers.

"Leave us alone until I call for you," Macbeth said to the attendant.

He said to the two murderers, "Was it not yesterday we spoke together?"

The First Murderer replied, "It was, so please your Highness."

"Have you thought about what I said to you then?" Macbeth asked. "I explained to you two that Banquo was your enemy and had plotted against you. Previously, you two had thought that it was I who was your enemy. I showed to both of you clear proof of these things the last time we met. I proved who deceived you, who thwarted you, who plotted against you, and other things that would convince even a half-wit and an insane person to believe 'Banquo is my enemy.'"

The First Murderer replied, "You made these things known to us."

"I did all that, and more," Macbeth said. "And now let us get to the point of this, our second meeting. Is your nature such that you can let this man's bad treatment of you two pass without your getting revenge? Are you made so meek by the Christian gospel that you will pray for this good man and for his children — this man whose heavy hand has brought you close to your grave and made beggars of your families?"

"We are men, my liege," the First Murderer said, "and as we are men, we will seek revenge."

"Yes, you are part of the many who are called men. Similarly, hounds and greyhounds, mongrels, spaniels, curs, shaggy dogs, longhaired water dogs, and dog-wolf mixes are all called dogs. However, dogs are classified by their traits. Some dogs are swift, some are slow, some guard the household, some are used in hunting, and so on. Each kind of dog has its gift that nature has given it, and so it can be distinguished from the other kinds of dog. This kind of list is more informative than a list that simply contains the names of various kinds of dogs. Similarly, men are classified by their traits. Where in the list of men appear you two? Are you in the worst rank of Mankind, or above the worst rank? Should I entrust you two with a plan that will get rid of Banquo? Should I entrust you two with a plan that will make you my friends? As long as Banquo lives, I am ill at ease, but after Banquo dies, I shall be perfectly happy."

The Second Murderer said, "I am a man who has been so badly treated by the world that in my anger I don't much care what I do as long as I get some revenge for how I have been treated."

The First Murderer said, "I am another such man. I am tired of the disasters I have suffered and I am tired of being the plaything of fate, and so I am willing to risk my life on the chance of improving my fortune. If I fail, I can but die."

"Both of you know that Banquo is your enemy?" Macbeth asked.

"Yes, we do," said the two murderers.

"Banquo is also my enemy," Macbeth said. "Every moment that he is alive creates a pain in my heart. As King, I could easily and openly have him killed and be able to justify the killing, yet I must not, because he and I have certain friends in common whom I must keep as friends but who would mourn his death even if the King himself had ordered it. That is why I need you two. I must keep my part in Banquo's death secret for various important reasons."

"We shall, my lord, perform what you command us," the Second Murderer said.

The First Murderer said, "Though our lives —"

Macbeth interrupted, "I can see that you are capable of doing what you promise to do. Within the next hour, I will tell you where you will hide in waiting for Banquo. I will give you the best information possible, including the best time to do what you have promised to do. This information comes from a man who well knows how to get information. This deed must be done tonight, and it must be done at some distance from the castle. Always remember that I must not be suspected of planning Banquo's death. In addition, so that this deed is accomplished perfectly, you must kill Fleance, Banquo's son. Fleance's death is as desired by me as is Banquo's death. Leave now, and make sure that you are resolved to carry out this plan. I will come to you soon."

Both murderers replied, "We are resolved to do what we have promised."

The two murderers left, and Macbeth said, "The plan is complete. Banquo, if your soul is going to go to Heaven, it must find its way there tonight."

— 3.2 —

Lady Macbeth asked a servant in the castle, "Has Banquo gone from court?"

The servant replied, "Yes, madam, but he returns again tonight."

"Tell the King that I would like to talk to him."

"Madam, I will."

The servant left the room.

Alone in the room, Lady Macbeth thought, *Nothing is gained; all is spent. We have gained nothing; we have spent all we had. We have gotten what we thought we desired, but it has brought us no happiness. We would have been better off if we had been murdered instead of us murdering King Duncan. We committed murder, seeking joy, but the result for us has not been joy.*

Seeing her husband enter the room, Lady Macbeth said, "Why do you reject company and stay alone by yourself? Your only companions are sad thoughts. These sad thoughts about the men you have murdered should die just like the murdered men. We can't fix what we have done; therefore, we ought not to think about it. What has been done will stay done."

"We have wounded the snake, but not killed it," Macbeth said. "The snake will heal and be healthy again, and its fangs will threaten us, its feeble enemy. I wish that reality would disintegrate; I wish that Heaven and Earth would both perish. Destruction would be better than the reality of my shaking with fear as I eat and the reality of my shaking with fear from nightmares as I sleep. I would be better off dead. It is better for me to lie with the dead, whom I sent to their peace so that I could gain power, than to be tortured with this restless madness. King Duncan is in his grave. He experienced life's fitful fever, but now he rests well. Treason has done its worst and killed him. Now, he is untouched by steel swords, deadly poison, Scottish traitors, and foreign armies — nothing can hurt him."

"My noble lord," Lady Macbeth said, "put on a happier face than the one you display now. Be lively and jovial among your guests tonight."

"I will," Macbeth replied, "and I hope that you will do the same. But let us talk a moment about Banquo. Honor him both with your eyes and your words. Show respect to him. We are still unsafe in our positions as King and Queen, and we must flatter him. We must wear a face that disguises what is in our hearts."

"You must stop talking and thinking like this."

"Dear wife," Macbeth said, "my mind is full of scorpions — it is dangerous and it hurts. As you know, Banquo and his son, Fleance, are still alive."

"Neither of them has been granted eternal life in this world."

"I take comfort in that fact," Macbeth said. "They can be killed. Be cheerful tonight. Before the bat takes its flight in the dark regions of our castle, before the winged beetle sounds the arrival of night for Hecate, goddess of witches, a deed of dreadful note shall be done."

"What's to be done?"

"I won't tell you, dearest darling, until the deed is done. Then you may applaud it. Come, darkness, blindfold the eyes of daylight, and with your bloody and invisible hand, tear to pieces that life that makes me pale with fear. The light is fading, and the crow is flying to its home. The good beings who are active in the daytime are beginning to droop and drowse, while the black agents that are active in the nighttime are awakening. You, wife, don't understand my words now, but wait a while longer. Evil beings can start out weak, but make themselves strong by doing more evil. Come with me now."

They left the room.

— 3.3 —

Three murderers, including the two murderers Macbeth had talked to earlier, stood together.

The First Murderer asked, "Who told you to join with us?"

"Macbeth," answered the Third Murderer.

"We need not mistrust him," the Second Murderer said. "He knows exactly what Macbeth told us to do and how Macbeth told us to do it."

"Then join with us," said the Second Murderer to the Third Murderer. "The setting Sun still sends forth some rays of light. Now travelers urge their horses to go faster so that they may soon reach an inn to stay at, and soon the man we have been waiting for will appear."

"I hear horses," the Third Murderer said.

The Third Murderer heard the voice of Banquo saying to a servant, "Give us a torch to light our way."

"This is the man we have been waiting for," the Second Murderer said. "Macbeth's other guests are already in the castle."

"They have dismounted from their horses," the First Murderer said.

"They are still about a mile from the castle," the Third Murderer said. "It is the custom for the servants to walk the horses by a longer route to the castle to cool them off, while the masters walk from here to the castle."

"I see a light!" the Second Murderer said.

Banquo and Fleance stood revealed by the light cast by the torch that Fleance carried.

"It is Banquo," the Third Murderer said.

"Get ready," the First Murderer said.

Banquo said, "It will rain tonight."

"Then let the rain come down," the First Murderer said.

The three murderers attacked, concentrating on Banquo, who was an older, experienced warrior and much more dangerous than his son. In the confusion, the First Murderer extinguished the torch and the darkness made seeing difficult.

"We are under attack!" Banquo shouted. A good father, he shouted, "Run, Fleance! Save yourself, and avenge me later!"

The three murderers succeeded in cutting down Banquo, but Fleance succeeded in escaping.

"Who put out the torch?" the Third Murderer asked.

"Wasn't that the right thing to do?" the First Murderer asked.

"We have killed Banquo only," the Third Murderer said. "His son has escaped."

"We have failed in half of our mission," the Second Murderer said.

"Let's leave," the First Murderer said, "and tell Macbeth what has happened."

— 3.4 —

In the great hall of the castle, a feast was set out on the long table. In the great hall were Macbeth, Lady Macbeth, Ross, Lennox, various other members of nobility, and many servants.

"Please sit down according to your degree of nobility, and welcome, all," Macbeth said.

"Thank you, your majesty," all of the lords replied.

"I myself shall be the humble host and mingle with all," Macbeth said. "For now my wife shall sit on her chair of state, and later we shall ask for her to mingle."

"Welcome all our friends for me, sir," Lady Macbeth said. "In my heart they are our friends and they are all welcome here."

The First Murderer appeared at the door.

Macbeth said to his wife, "Our guests return your friendship in their hearts."

Then he said to the guests, "Both sides — the Queen and the nobility — are equal in giving friendship. I will sit here in the midst of our guests. Be happy, all. Soon we will all drink a toast around the table."

Seeing the First Murderer, Macbeth walked to the door and said quietly to him, "There's blood on your face."

The First Murderer replied, "It is Banquo's blood."

"I prefer it to be on your outside than in his inside," Macbeth said. "Is he dead?"

"My lord, his throat is cut — I cut it for him."

"You are the best of the cutthroats," Macbeth said. "The person who cut Fleance's throat is also good. If you did that, too, you have no equal."

"Most royal sir, Fleance escaped."

"Then I still have a problem that causes me fits," Macbeth said. "If Fleance had also been murdered, my problems would be over. I would be as solid as marble, as firmly based as a boulder, as freely and widely ranging as the air. Instead, I continue to be shut up in a claustrophobic place and assailed by doubts and fears. But is Banquo truly dead?"

"Yes, my good lord. His corpse lies in a ditch, and his head bears twenty gashes, each one of them fatal."

"Thank you for that," Macbeth said. "The grown serpent is dead. The young serpent that escaped will grow up and become poisonous. At present it is not dangerous. Leave now. Tomorrow we will speak together again."

The First Murderer left, and Macbeth went back to his guests and his wife.

Lady Macbeth quietly said to him, "My royal lord, you have not been making our guests feel welcome. Unless the host makes the guests feel welcome, it is as if they are paying customers rather than honored guests. If our guests merely wanted to satisfy their hunger, they could do that at their own homes. Etiquette and welcome provide the sauce to a feast. Without proper etiquette and without a proper welcoming of guests, a feast is lacking."

Macbeth said to Lady Macbeth, "Sweet remembrancer!"

Unseen by anyone, the bloody ghost of Banquo entered the great hall and sat down in the chair reserved for Macbeth at the long table.

Macbeth turned to his guests and said, "May everyone have good appetite, good digestion, and good health."

He added, "Here under this roof we would have nearly all of Scotland's nobility if only Banquo, who is endowed with grace, were present. I would prefer to criticize him for forgetting to show up on time rather than to pity him for any mishap that may have occurred to him."

Ross said, "Banquo's absence means that he has failed to keep his promise to be present. If it would please your highness, please sit down and favor us with your company."

"All the seats are taken," Macbeth said.

"Here is a seat that is reserved for you, sir," Lennox said.

"Where?"

"Here, my good lord."

Banquo's ghost turned in the chair indicated and looked at Macbeth, who looked at the chair and saw seated on it the bloody ghost of Banquo. Startled, Macbeth drew back, his hand on his sword hilt.

"What is it that has startled your highness?" Lennox asked.

"Which of you have done this?" Macbeth shouted.

The nobles and Lady Macbeth could not see the ghost, and they did not know that Macbeth was referring to the wounds that had bloodied Banquo's head — Macbeth was making a feeble attempt to have someone else blamed for the wounds.

"What, my good lord?" Lennox asked.

Macbeth said to the ghost that none but he could see, "You cannot say that I did it — don't shake your gory locks of hair at me!"

Seeing Macbeth agitated, Ross said, "Gentlemen, stand up. His highness is not well."

Lady Macbeth tried to bring order out of chaos by saying, "Sit, worthy friends. The King is often like this, and he has been this way since his youth. Please, stay seated. His illness will end quickly. He will be himself again in a moment. If you stare at him, you will make him worse and extend the length of time his fit lasts. Eat now, and ignore the King."

To her husband, she said under her breath, "Are you a man?"

"Yes," Macbeth said to her. "I am a bold man, but I am looking at something that might make even Satan afraid."

"Stuff and nonsense," Lady Macbeth replied. "This is something conjured by your fear. This is like the dagger you hallucinated that you told me led you to

King Duncan's bedchamber. These startled outbursts of yours would be suitable for a child sitting in front of a fireplace and listening to a woman tell a story that had been told to her by her grandmother. These startled outbursts of yours are not true fear. You should be ashamed of yourself. Why are you making such wild faces! You are looking at nothing but a chair!"

Macbeth looked again, and again he saw the bloody ghost of Banquo seated on the chair. He said to his wife, "Look! How can you say that nothing is there except a chair?"

Then he said to Banquo's ghost, "Why should I care anything about you? I can see you moving your head. If you can do that, then speak to me. If tombs and graves are going to eject their corpses instead of hiding them, then the corpses ought to be eaten by birds and hidden in their stomachs."

The ghost of Banquo vanished.

"Has your fear turned you into a weak woman?" Lady Macbeth asked her husband.

"Just as surely as I am standing here, I saw a ghost."

"You should be ashamed," Lady Macbeth said.

"Blood has been spilled before now — back in the ancient times before we had laws to restrain people and make them gentler," Macbeth said. "Even now, terrible murders are committed that are horrifying to hear about. But it used to be true that when a man's brains were dashed out of his skull, the man would die and stay dead. That is no longer true. Now the dead man will rise and walk again despite twenty mortal wounds to his head. What I just saw is more abnormal than even murder."

Macbeth had much recovered from seeing the ghost, and Lady Macbeth said to him, "My worthy lord, your noble friends lack your company."

"I do forget," Macbeth said. "Do not mind me, my most worthy friends. I have a strange infirmity, but people who know me well don't fuss about it. I wish love and health to all of you. I will sit down. Give me some wine — fill the goblet full. I drink to the general joy of the whole table and to our dear friend Banquo, whom we miss. All of us wish that he were here. To all, and to Banquo, let us drink."

"Hear, hear," said the nobles.

As Macbeth and the others drank a toast, the ghost of Banquo entered the great hall again.

Catching sight of the ghost, Macbeth shouted, "Go away! Get out of my sight! Let the dirt cover you in your grave! Your bones have no marrow! Your blood is cold! Your eyes are blind although you glare at me!"

Lady Macbeth said to the nobles, "Think of this, good peers, only as a common effect of my husband's illness. It is not dangerous, although it spoils the pleasure of the feast."

Macbeth shouted at the ghost, "I am brave. What any man dares, I dare. Approach me in the shape of a rugged Russian bear, a thick-hided rhinoceros armed with a horn, or an Asian tiger. Take any shape but the shape you have now, and I will not tremble in fear. Or be alive again and challenge me to fight you in a deserted place. If I stay home and tremble in fear, then say that I have the courage of the doll of a girl. Get away from me, horrible shadow! Leave now, unreal mockery! Go!"

The ghost of Banquo vanished.

Macbeth said, "Now that the ghost has left, I am a man again. Please, everyone, sit down."

"Your actions have ruined the feast and made everyone uncomfortable," Lady Macbeth said to her husband.

"How is it possible that such visions can appear and come over us like a cloud without everyone being amazed?" Macbeth said to his wife. "I see such visions and am no longer myself — my face turns white with fear. But you see such visions and your cheeks stay red with their natural color. When I see such visions, I feel like a stranger to my true — that is, my brave — nature."

Ross, who had overheard the conversation between Macbeth and Lady Macbeth, said, "What visions, my lord?"

Lady Macbeth said to the nobles, "I beg you, don't speak to the King. He grows worse and worse, and question enrages him. At once, please leave and good night. Do not take the time to leave in the order of your rank, but please leave at once."

Lennox said, "Good night, and better health attend his majesty!"

"A kind good night to all!" Lady Macbeth said.

The nobles departed with much to talk about.

Macbeth and Lady Macbeth stood alone in the great hall.

"Blood will have blood," Macbeth said. "The murdered will have their revenge. Gravestones have been said to move and trees to speak, all to bring murderers to justice. Predictions and psychic evidence reveal murderers. Even the actions of magpies and jackdaws and crows have brought forth evidence to reveal a murderer. What time is it?"

"It is so close to morning that it is difficult to tell whether it is night or morning," Lady Macbeth replied.

"Macduff declines to come to me when I send for him. What is your opinion of that?"

"Did you send to him, sir?"

"I am reporting to you what I have heard, but I will send for him. Actually, I have already sent for him once — he refused to come and attend our banquet. In every noble's household I have at least one servant whom I pay to be a spy. Early tomorrow, I will seek the Weird Sisters. I want more information. I am resolved to know the worst even if I have to consult evil witches to know it. I will satisfy my curiosity — to me, nothing is more important than that I get the information I seek. I have waded into a river of blood. I have waded so far and so deep into the river that I might as well keep going rather than return to the bank from which I started. I have in mind strange plots, and I intend to act on them before I think about them too much."

"You need to get some sleep," Lady Macbeth said.

"Let's go to bed," Macbeth agreed. "My vision of the ghost was simply the fear of a novice to the doing of evil. I need to be more evil and do more evil. I am still much too inexperienced in the doing of dirty deeds."

— 3.5 —

On a heath below a lightning storm, the three Weird Sisters met Hecate, the goddess of witches. Hecate was not happy. Thunder sounded during their meeting.

"Greetings, Hecate," the First Witch said. "You look angry."

"Haven't I just reason to be angry?" Hecate replied. "You hags don't know your place. You are overly bold. How dare you tempt Macbeth with riddles to commit murder without my participation? I am your master, I am the secret plotter of all harms, and I *will* have a part in corrupting Macbeth's soul. Macbeth is nothing but a wayward son. He is spiteful and angry, and he loves himself, not you. But now you can make amends to me for your wayward actions. In the morning, meet me at the pit that leads down to Acheron, one of the rivers of Hell. Macbeth will go there in the morning to seek you to learn about his future. Bring with you your cauldron and the ingredients for your spells and your charms. I will fly in the sky tonight, working on dismal and deadly business. An airy drop of heavy significance hangs from the Moon; I will catch it before it falls to Earth. Through the use of magic, I will use that drop to raise unnatural visions to mislead Macbeth further along the path of his ruin. After he sees my visions, Macbeth will spurn fate, scorn death, and value false hopes more than he values wisdom, gifts from Almighty God, and reasonable fears. As all of you know, overconfidence is the chief enemy of mortals. Death is coming soon for Macbeth, but he will not know it."

Nearby, music played and the words "Come away ... come away" filled the air.

Hecate said, "My familiar spirit — a demon — is calling for me. It sits on a foggy cloud and waits for me to come."

Hecate flew away, and the First Witch said, "Come, let's make haste — Hecate will soon be back again."

The three Weird Sisters left.

— 3.6 —

At Forres, the site of the late King Duncan's castle, Lennox and another lord spoke together.

"Your opinions and mine are in agreement," Lennox said. "Strange things have been occurring. The good King Duncan died, and Macbeth pitied him, so he says. The valiant Banquo walked at night, and Banquo died, and Macbeth pitied him, so he says. You can say, if you like, that Fleance killed his father, Banquo. How do we know that he did that? Because Fleance fled following the murder he had committed, so Macbeth says. It is monstrous for a son to kill a father, so Macbeth says. Fleance did kill his father, so Macbeth says. And Malcolm and Donalbain did kill their father, so Macbeth says. Damned deeds! Macbeth grieved, so he says. He grieved so much, he says, that he killed the King's bodyguards, who were drunk and asleep. Wasn't that a noble deed for Macbeth to do? He says so, and he also says that it was a good deed, too. To hear the bodyguards deny that they had murdered the King would have angered any man, so Macbeth says. Macbeth has handled all these matters well — so he says. You may believe Macbeth's words if you like — but I know that you do not, and neither do I! I think that if Macbeth had power over Malcolm and Donalbain and power over Fleance, they would soon be murdered and so

41

learn the consequences of murdering their fathers, as Macbeth would say. May Heaven never allow Macbeth to have power over King Duncan's sons and over Banquo's son!

"By the way, I hear that Macduff is in Macbeth's disfavor because Macduff speaks too frankly and too openly. Can you tell me where Macduff is these days?"

The lord replied, "Macduff has gone to visit Malcolm, who — being the late King Duncan's oldest son — ought to be King. The tyrant Macbeth withholds from Malcolm what is his by birthright. Malcolm now lives in the court of the King of England: Edward the Confessor. This King graciously welcomed Malcolm and treats him with great respect despite Malcolm's misfortunes and the deprivation of the crown that is rightfully his. Macduff wants Edward the Confessor to call to arms the people in Northumberland, which borders Scotland, so that its governor the Earl Siward can lead them into battle against Macbeth. If an army is raised to fight against Macbeth, and if the great and good God is willing, as He must be, we will again have food on our tables, we will again be able to sleep easily at night, we will again be able to attend a King's feast without fear of being murdered, we will again be able to support a King with our own free will instead of supporting the King out of fear of what would happen if we did not support that King, and we will again be able to receive the honors due to patriotic men. Under the tyranny of Macbeth, we can no longer do or enjoy any of these things.

"Also, Macbeth has heard about Macduff. Macbeth knows that a rebellion is forming, and he is preparing for war."

"Did Macbeth order Macduff to come to his banquet?" Lennox asked.

"Yes," the lord answered, "and Macduff told Macbeth's messenger, 'Sir, I will not go to Macbeth's banquet.' The unhappy messenger turned his back on Macduff as if to say, 'You will regret the time that you gave me this answer to take to Macbeth.'"

"The messenger's action may well convince Macduff to be cautious in opposing Macbeth and to keep away from Scotland — the wrath of Macbeth is terrible and something to be feared," Lennox said. "It is possible that Macduff could stay in exile and not advocate that an army oppose Macbeth. I wish that an angel would fly to Macduff and tell him that the quicker an army opposes

Macbeth the better it will be for Scotland. The removal of the tyrant will be a blessing for our country."

The lord replied, "I would like to send my own prayers with that angel."

CHAPTER 4: PILED HIGHER AND DEEPER

— 4.1 —

The three Weird Sisters stood around a boiling cauldron in a cave. Outside a lightning storm raged.

"Three times the striped cat has mewed," the First Witch said.

"Three times, and the hedgehog has whined once," said the Second Witch.

"Harpier, my familiar, cries, 'It is time … it is time," the Third Witch said.

The First Witch said, "Round about the cauldron go; in the pot poisoned entrails throw. First to be boiled is a toad that sweated venom for thirty-one days as it sat under a cold rock."

All the witches chanted together, "Double, double, toil and trouble; fire burn, and cauldron bubble."

The Second Witch said, "Slice of a swampland snake, in the cauldron boil and bake; eye of newt and toe of frog, wool of bat and tongue of dog, adder's forked tongue and blind-snake's poisonous sting, lizard's leg, and owlet's wing, for a charm of powerful trouble, like a Hell-broth boil and bubble."

All the witches chanted together, "Double, double, toil and trouble; fire burn, and cauldron bubble."

The Third Witch said, "Scale of a dragon, tooth of a wolf, mummy of a witch, gullet and throat of a ravenous sea-shark, root of hemlock dug up in the dark, liver of a blaspheming Jew, gall of a goat, and twigs of the poisonous yew tree sliced off during the eclipse of the Moon, nose of a Turk and lips of a Tartar, and finger of a newborn babe who is damned because its mother, a whore, gave birth to it in a ditch and strangled it before it was baptized. Throw these into the cauldron and make the gruel thick and viscous. Add the entrails of a tiger to the ingredients of our cauldron."

All the witches chanted together, "Double, double, toil and trouble; fire burn, and cauldron bubble."

The Second Witch said, "Cool it with a baboon's blood, and then the charm is firm and the opposite of good."

Hecate entered the cave and examined the gruel in the cauldron. She said to the Weird Sisters, "Well done. I commend you for the pains that you have

44

taken to brew this evil charm, and all of you will share in its gains. And now about the cauldron sing, like elves and fairies in a ring, enchanting all that you put in.”

All danced and sang around the cauldron, and the charm was ready for use when Macbeth arrived.

The Second Witch felt sudden pain — a harbinger of approaching evil — and said, “By the pricking of my thumbs, something wicked this way comes.”

Her words were true now, but if she had spoken them before the Three Witches had tempted Macbeth, they would not have been true. Earlier, Macbeth had been a patriot and a hero, but now he was a regicide and a tyrant.

Hecate left, leaving the Three Witches in the cave awaiting Macbeth.

The Second Witch ordered, “Open, locks, to whoever knocks!”

Leaving Lennox outside, Macbeth entered the cave and said, “What are you doing, you secret, black, and midnight hags?”

The Three Witches replied, “A deed without a name. No name exists for what we are doing.”

Macbeth said to the witches, “I order you in the name of Satan or whatever other powers you serve to answer my questions no matter by which means you acquire the necessary knowledge to reply. Even if you untie the winds and let them blow against the churches, even if you make the foamy waves batter and sink ships and drown sailors, even if you beat down crops of food and blow down trees, even if you topple palaces and steeples, even if you turn nature into chaos so that no seeds ever again bring forth life, even if you cause so much destruction that chaos itself is sickened, I demand that you tell me the answers to the questions I will ask you.”

The First Witch said, “Speak.”

The Second Witch said, “Demand.”

The Third Witch said, “We will answer.”

The First Witch asked, “Tell us whether you would rather hear the answers from our own mouths, or from the mouths of our masters?”

“Call your masters,” Macbeth ordered. “Let me see them.”

The First Witch chanted, “Pour into the flame the blood of a sow that has eaten her nine piglets. Pour into the flame the grease that has dripped from the skin-sores of the decomposed corpse of a murderer who has been hanging from a gibbet for days.”

All the witches chanted, "Come, high spirit or low spirit; yourself and your knowledge deftly show!"

Thunder sounded, and the first apparition — a male head wearing a helmet — rose from the cauldron.

Macbeth began to speak to the apparition, "Tell me, unknown power —"

The First Witch told Macbeth, "He knows your thought. Hear his speech, but say nothing to him."

The first apparition said, "Macbeth! Macbeth! Macbeth! Beware Macduff! Beware the Thane of Fife! Dismiss me. Enough."

Macbeth replied, "Whatever you are, thank you for your warning. I have long been suspicious of Macduff. But one word more."

The First Witch said, "He will not obey your orders."

The first apparition disappeared into the cauldron, and the First Witch said, "Here's another that is more powerful than the first."

Thunder sounded, and the second apparition — a child covered with blood — rose from the cauldron.

The second apparition called, "Macbeth! Macbeth! Macbeth!"

Macbeth replied, "Had I three ears, I would listen to your words with all three."

The second apparition said, "Be bloody, bold, and resolute; laugh to scorn the power of man, for none of woman born shall harm Macbeth."

The second apparition disappeared into the cauldron.

Macbeth said, "Then I can let Macduff live because why should I fear him? But nevertheless I will take steps to ensure that Macduff shall do me no harm. Macduff shall not live. Then I can tell my white-hearted fear that it has nothing to be afraid of, and I can sleep even when the sky thunders."

Thunder sounded, and the third apparition — a child wearing a crown and holding a tree branch in his hand — rose from the cauldron.

Macbeth asked, "Who is this who rises like the son of a King and wears upon his baby-brow the round and top — the crown — of sovereignty?"

The Three Witches said to Macbeth, "Listen to the apparition but do not speak to it."

The third apparition said to Macbeth, "Have the courage of a lion, and be proud. Don't concern yourself about those who resent you and your rule and suffer under it. Don't concern yourself about conspirers. Macbeth shall never be conquered until the great Birnam Forest marches twelve miles to your castle on the high Dunsinane hill."

The third apparition disappeared into the cauldron.

Macbeth said, "That will never happen. Who can make a forest uproot itself and march for twelve miles? These are good omens for me! Banquo, you rebelled against death by appearing to me as a ghost. Never rise again until Birnam Forest rises up and marches against me. I, the King, will live until I die of old age and natural causes. Yet I still want to know one thing more: Shall Banquo's descendants ever reign in this kingdom?"

The Weird Sisters replied, "Seek to know no more."

"I will know the answer to my question!" Macbeth said. "If you do not answer, may an eternal curse fall upon you! Tell me! Why is the cauldron sinking? What music am I hearing?"

The music of oboes sounded.

The First Witch ordered, "Show him!"

The Second Witch ordered, "Show him!"

The Third Witch ordered, "Show him!"

All three Weird Sisters ordered, "Show his eyes, and grieve his heart; come like shadows, then depart!"

Spirits showed themselves in the forms of eight Kings. The eighth King had a mirror in his hand. The ghost of Banquo also appeared.

Macbeth shouted, "You look like the ghost of Banquo! Go away!"

Macbeth then shouted at the first King, "Your crown sears my eyeballs."

Then he shouted at the second King, "Your hair, your brow that is crowned with gold, resembles those of the first King! And the third King resembles you!"

Macbeth then shouted at the three Weird Sisters, "Why do you show me this! I see a fourth King! Eyes, jump out of your sockets! What, will the line of Kings stretch out to the crack of doom? I see another and another King! A seventh! I don't want to see any more Kings, and yet an eighth King appears, holding a mirror in which I see many more Kings, some of whom are carrying coronation emblems that show that they are Kings of multiple countries! This is a horrible sight for me! Banquo — his head bloody — smiles at me and points to his descendants, all of them Kings!"

The apparitions vanished.

Macbeth asked, "Is all of this true?"

The First Witch answered, "Yes, all that you have seen is true. You are acting like a person in shock, but we Weird Sisters will cheer you up and entertain you. I will charm music out of the air and my sisters will dance. We want you, great King, to kindly say that we welcomed you."

The witches danced until Hecate showed herself, and then they and Hecate vanished.

Macbeth listened a moment, heard only the galloping of horses, and said, "Where are the Weird Sisters? Gone? Let this evil day be forever a day of ill omen in the calendar! Lennox, come here!"

Lennox entered the cave and asked, "What are your orders for me?"

"Saw you the Weird Sisters?" Macbeth asked.

"No, my lord," Lennox replied.

"Didn't they pass by you?"

"No, indeed not, my lord."

Macbeth said, "The air that the three Weird Sisters ride upon is infected with corruption, and everyone who trusts them is damned. I heard horses galloping. Who was it who came here?"

"A few men came here to tell you that Macduff has fled to England."

"England!"

"Yes, my good lord."

"Macduff timely anticipated what I was going to do to him," Macbeth said. "Anyone who forms a plan ought to act immediately on it. From this moment on, I will do so: Whenever I form a plan in my heart, I will act on it and bring it to fruition. I will start to do that right now: I will attack Macduff's castle at Fife, and I will kill his wife, his children, and anyone unfortunate enough to be related to him. I won't boast of deeds not done; instead, I will ensure that this deed is done before I change my mind. I will also no longer seek to see the apparitions of the Weird Sisters! Where are the messengers? Take me to them."

— 4.2 —

At Macduff's castle in Fife, Lady Macduff, her young son by her side, talked with Ross.

"What did my husband do to make him flee from Scotland?" asked Lady Macduff.

"You must have patience, madam," Ross replied.

"My husband had no patience. His flight was madness. His actions did not make him a traitor, but his fearful flight makes him appear to be a traitor."

"You don't know whether it was his wisdom or his fear that made him flee," Ross said.

"How could it be wisdom," Lady Macduff said, "to leave his wife, his children, and his possessions in a place from which he himself flees in fear? He does not love us. He lacks the natural instincts that even animals have. The poor mother wren, the smallest of birds, will fight an owl to protect her young ones in her nest. Fear, not love, rules my husband's actions. His flight is against all reason, and so it is not wise, either."

"My dearest cousin, I advise you to control yourself. Your husband is noble, wise, and judicious, and he best knows the disorders present now in Scotland. I dare not speak much further, but cruel are the times when men are called traitors and do not know why they are called traitors. We are so fearful that we believe rumors, and yet we do not know what it is we fear. We seem to be floating upon a wild and violent sea that tosses us one way and then the other. I take my leave of you. Soon I shall return. When the times are at their worst, they cease becoming worse and may even improve to where they were before. My pretty cousin, God's blessing be upon you!"

"My son has a father, and yet he is fatherless because his father has forsaken him."

Ross replied, "I am so much a fool that should I stay longer, I would cry, and that would be my disgrace and your discomfort; therefore, I take my leave at once."

Ross departed.

Lady Macduff said to her young son, "Your father is dead. What will you do now? How will you live?" She expected bad news and hoped to prepare her son for it by talking to him now.

"As birds do, mother."

"What, with worms and flies?"

"With what I get, mother. That is how birds live."

"My son, you would make a poor bird," Lady Macduff said. "You would not know enough to be afraid of the nets and snares used to catch birds."

"Why should I, mother? If I am a poor bird, hunters will not want to catch me. And you are wrong about my father — he is not dead."

"Yes, he is dead," Lady Macbeth lied, hoping to prepare her son for whatever bad news would arrive. "What will you do to get a new father?"

"What will you do to get a new husband?"

"Why, I can buy twenty husbands at any market."

"Then you will buy them to sell again at a profit."

"You are speaking with all your wit. Truly, you have wit enough to suit you."

"Was my father a traitor, mother?"

"Yes, he was."

"What is a traitor?

"Why, one who swears and lies — one who swears an oath of allegiance but does not keep his oath."

"And be all traitors who do so?"

"Every one who does so is a traitor, and must be hanged."

"And must they all be hanged who swear and lie?"

"Every one."

"Who must hang them?"

"The honest men must hang them."

"Then the liars and swearers are fools," her son said, "for there are liars and swearers enough to beat the honest men and hang them."

"That is all too true," Lady Macduff said, "and all too cynical for a boy as young as you to believe. God help you, you poor monkey! How will you get a new father?"

"If my father were dead, you would weep for him unless you were going to marry someone new. Since you are not weeping, that is a good sign that either he is not dead or I will soon have a new father."

"Poor prattler, how you talk!"

A messenger entered the room and said to Lady Macduff, "God bless you, fair lady! You do not know me, but I know your rank. I fear that some danger does quickly approach you. If you will take a simple, plain man's advice, you will flee immediately. Do not stay here with your children. Flee! I am sorry to have to frighten you like this, but I do not want something much more cruel to happen to you and your children. If you stay here, you will suffer much cruelty — it quickly approaches you! Heaven help you! I dare not stay here any longer!"

The messenger left in a hurry.

"Where should I flee to?" Lady Macduff said. "I have done no harm. But I am in this Earthly world where to do harm is often considered worthy of praise and where to do good is often considered the action of a fool. In such a world, what good does it do for a woman to say, 'I have done no harm'?"

Murderers entered the room.

"Who are you?" Lady Macduff asked.

"Where is your husband?" a murderer asked.

"I hope that he is in no place so unsanctified that people like you can find him."

"He's a traitor," a murderer said.

Lady Macduff's young son shouted, "You're lying, you shaggy-haired villain!"

"Runt!" the murderer shouted and stabbed the boy, who shouted, "He has killed me, mother. Run!"

Lady Macduff ran away from the murderers and screamed, "Murder!" She did not run fast enough.

— 4.3 —

Malcolm and Macduff were meeting outside the palace of the King of England. Malcolm's bodyguards were near.

Malcolm said, "Let us find some shade and mourn for Scotland there."

Macduff replied, "Let us instead wield deadly swords and like good men defend Scotland and wrest it from the tyrant, who with each new day makes new widows howl with grief and new orphans cry. Each day, the tyrant creates new sorrows that slap Heaven in the face — the slaps make Heaven cry out in pain and in sympathy for Scotland."

"I will mourn whatever evils I believe to have occurred," Malcolm said. "I will believe what I learn to be the truth, and whatever evils I can avenge, I will avenge — at the right time. The things you have been telling me may very well be true. This tyrant, whose name blisters our tongues when we speak it, was once thought to be good. You used to think highly of him. He has done nothing to harm you that I am aware of. I am young, but I am old enough to realize that you may be seeking to earn favor with Macbeth by doing harm to me. Some think that it is wise to offer up a weak, poor, innocent lamb to appease an angry god. You may think it wise to offer up me to appease an angry tyrant."

"I am not treacherous," Macduff replied.

"But Macbeth is. Even a good and virtuous man may think it wise to obey the orders of a cruel tyrant. But I may be wrong in my suspicions of you. I may suspect you, but yet you may be a good man. Angels are still bright, although the brightest angel — Lucifer — became evil and fell from Paradise. Evil men seek to have the appearance of good men. Good men have that appearance naturally. Therefore, an evil man and a good man may have the same appearance but not the same nature."

"I wanted you to gather an army to fight Macbeth, but I have lost all hope of that ever happening," Macduff said.

"You have your doubts about me," Malcolm said, "and I have my doubts about you. Why did you leave your wife and children behind without defenses in the dangerous land of Scotland — you love them, don't you? If you are an agent of Macbeth, you could leave them behind without worry. I ask this because I want to protect myself, and by being cautious and fearing plots I can best defend myself. Despite my cautiousness, you may be a good and just man."

"Bleed, poor Scotland, bleed!" Macduff mourned. "Tyrant, do your worst and do it openly because good people dare not oppose you. Enjoy the fruits of your evil, and boast about them. Farewell, lord Malcolm. I would not be the villain whom you think I am even if I were offered everything that the tyrant controls and all of the rich East as well."

"Don't be offended," Malcolm said. "I am not entirely convinced that you are an agent of Macbeth. I believe that Scotland sinks exhausted beneath the yoke the tyrant has put on it. Scotland weeps, it bleeds, and each day a new gash is added to her wounds. I think that many hands would be uplifted to fight for me and give me my rightful throne of Scotland. The gracious Edward the Confessor has offered thousands of soldiers to me to lead against Macbeth. However, once I have the tyrant's head under my boot or displayed at the end of my sword, Scotland will suffer worse and in more varied ways than it ever did under the tyrant."

"Who would bring such woes to Scotland?" Macduff asked.

"I would," Malcolm replied. "I know that in myself are all the many vices. Once I am in a position of power and able to enjoy my vices openly, black Macbeth will seem as pure as snow, and the citizens of Scotland will regard him as a lamb in comparison with me."

"No one can ever be as evil as Macbeth — not even a devil damned in Hell."

"I know that Macbeth is bloody, licentious, avaricious, false, deceitful, violent, malicious, and an enthusiastic participant of every sin that has a name. However, I have no limit to my lust. Scotland's wives, daughters, matrons, and maidens could not fill up the cistern of my lust. Anyone who tried to restrain the satisfaction of my lust I would strike down. It is better that Macbeth rule Scotland than that I do."

"Boundless lust in a man's nature is a kind of tyranny," Macduff replied. "It has caused many Kings to be removed from their thrones. Nevertheless, return to Scotland, oust Macbeth, and become King. You can satisfy your great lust in secret and appear to be virtuous in public. You can fool the Scots. Scotland has many women who would be willing enough to satisfy your lust. You cannot be so lustful as to run out of women who will willingly sleep with a King if they find out you want them."

"I also have in my character a greed without end for land and possessions. I would seize the land of the nobles. I would seize jewels and castles. The more land and possessions I seize, the more I would want. I would create false justifications to seize the land and possessions of good and loyal Scots — I would destroy them just so I can have their wealth."

"The evil of avarice is worse than the evil of lust. Lust will be less prevalent as you grow old, but greed can stay with you all your life. Like lust, greed has caused subjects to rebel against and kill many Kings. However, this does not mean you should not return to Scotland and become King. The royal lands and wealth are so great that they ought to satisfy your greed. Scotland can endure your vices if you have virtues to go with them."

"I have no virtues," Malcolm said. "I care nothing about justice, truth, temperance, stableness, bounty, perseverance, mercy, humility, devotion, patience, courage, fortitude. The people of Scotland will find no trace of these virtues in me, but they will find an abundance of each kind of vice in me. If I had the power to act on all my wishes, I would pour virtues into Hell so that they would be extinguished, I would turn universal peace into universal war, and I would take all unity on Earth and tear it to pieces."

"I mourn for Scotland!" Macduff said.

"If such a one be fit to govern, speak up. I am as I have spoken."

"Fit to govern!" Macduff said. "You are not fit to live! Our nation is miserable. A tyrant who lacks the true title to the throne and yet rules with a bloody scepter now governs Scotland. You are the rightful King of Scotland, and yet if your words are true you are unfit to rule and ought to be kept away from the throne. Your evil character would scandalize your ancestors. Your royal father was a most sainted King. The Queen who gave birth to you was oftener upon her knees praying than she was on her feet. Each day she lived, she prepared herself for residence in Paradise. Farewell to you! The evils that you say you are guilty of now make me an exile from my own country. I have no hope for Scotland. My hope ends here."

"Macduff, this love you have for Scotland shows that you are noble and have integrity," Malcolm said. "I have banished my suspicions about you. I know now that you are truthful and honorable. Many times has devil-like Macbeth tried to trick me and get me within his grasp. Because of this, I am not hasty to believe people. But now, let God witness that we shall work together. I will do as you wish and free Scotland. Know also that I take back my 'confession' of my 'vices.' I did not tell you the truth about the kind of person I am. The vices that I said are part of my character are in reality strangers to me. I am a virgin and have not sexually known a woman. I have never committed perjury. I scarcely value my own possessions, much less those of other people. I would not betray one devil to another devil. I love the truth as much as I love my life. My only lies are the ones I told you just now to test you and ensure that you were not an evil man who obeys the orders of Macbeth. I am yours to guide and Scotland's to command. In fact, before you arrived here, Old Siward with ten thousand soldiers gathered into an army was already coming here to be led in war against Macbeth. Now you and I will march together. I pray that our chance of success will equal the justice of our cause."

Macduff said nothing.

Malcolm asked him, "Why are you silent?"

"To hear such welcome things immediately after hearing such unwelcome things makes it difficult to know what to say."

A doctor walked up to Malcolm and Macduff.

"We will speak together at more length soon," Malcolm said to Macduff. Then he said to the doctor, "Is Edward the Confessor coming out?"

"Yes, sir," the doctor said. "Many wretchedly ill people await his cure by touch. Their illness cannot be cured by medical science, but when the King touches them, his touch heals their illness — such is his gift from Heaven."

"I thank you, doctor," Malcolm said.

The doctor departed.

"What is the disease he means?" Macduff asked.

"It is called the King's evil by most people because the King can cure it by the laying on of hands," Malcolm said. Others call it scrofula. I have often seen the good King Edward the Confessor cure it with a most miraculous work. What prayers he makes to Heaven, he alone knows, but strangely afflicted people, swollen and ulcerous, pitiful to the eye, with no hope of being cured by doctors, he cures. He prays as he hangs a golden coin around their necks, and it is said that when a King of England dies he passes on this gift to the next King. Along with this Heavenly gift, he has others, including the gift of prophecy. These gifts and other blessings show that he is full of grace and loved by God."

Ross walked up to Malcolm and Macduff.

Macduff asked Malcolm, "Who is this man coming toward us?"

"Judging by his clothing, a Scotsman, but I don't know him."

Now recognizing Ross, Macduff said to him, "My noble cousin, welcome."

Malcolm said, "I recognize him now. I pray to God that soon the circumstances that make us strangers will no longer exist. If I had not been exiled from Scotland for so long, I would have recognized Ross immediately."

Overhearing Malcolm's prayer, Ross said, "Sir, amen."

"Is the situation in Scotland still the same?" Malcolm asked.

"Pity our poor country!" Ross said, "It is almost afraid to look at itself. It should not be called our mother at this time, but rather our grave. No one smiles except those who are too ignorant or too stupid to know what is happening. Sighs and groans and shrieks rend the air, but they are now so common that they are no longer noticed. Violent sorrow is now a common experience. Death is so common that no one asks any more for whom the death bell tolls — someone is always dying and it is impossible to keep up to date on who is dead. The life of a good man is so short that the man dies before the flower in his cap dies. Good men die before they grow ill; they do not die of sickness of body."

"Your story is eloquently told, and it is true," Macduff said.

Malcolm asked, "What's the newest grief?"

"News of grief that is even an hour old is old news. Every minute a new cause for grieving pushes aside the old cause," Ross said.

"How is my wife?" Macduff asked.

Ross knew that Lady Macduff had been murdered, but he was reluctant to convey such bad news to her husband, so he replied, "Why, well."

"And all my children?"

"Well, too."

"The tyrant Macbeth has not battered at their peace and attacked them?"

Ross replied, "No; they were at peace when I did leave them." He thought, *That is partially true. It is false that Macbeth has not attacked them, but it is true that they were at peace when I left them — they were peacefully lying in their graves.*

Suspicious at Ross' obvious reluctance at answering his questions, Macduff said, "Be not a niggard of your speech. How are they?"

Still not willing to tell Macduff the truth and wanting to be sure that Malcolm would attack Macbeth, Ross replied, "When I came here to give you the bad news about Scotland, news that saddens me, I heard a rumor that many men were arming themselves in order to fight against Macbeth. I personally saw Macbeth's army on the march, and so I believe the rumor I heard. Now is the time for you, Malcolm, to help. Your presence in Scotland would create soldiers and would inspire even our women to fight to get rid of Macbeth and the distresses he inflicts upon them."

"They shall be comforted," Malcolm said. "We are going to Scotland. Edward the Confessor has given us the use of an army led by Old Siward. The Christian nations do not have a more experienced or more successful soldier."

"I wish that I could answer this comforting good news with news like it," Ross said, "but I have words that should be howled out in the desert air, where no one can hear them."

"Which person do such words concern?" Macduff asked. "Do they affect all Scots or just one Scot?"

"The news grieves all good Scots," Ross said, "but it will especially grieve you."

"If the grief be mine, keep it not from me. Quickly let me have it," Macduff said.

"Let not your ears despise my tongue forever," Ross said. "My tongue will speak words that will scar your ears."

"I can guess what you are going to say," Macduff said.

Ross told him what Macbeth had done: "Macbeth attacked your castle and savagely slaughtered your wife and children. If I were to give you specific details, your grief would cause your corpse to be added to the pile of dead bodies."

Macduff was silent.

Shocked, Malcolm said, "Merciful Heaven! Don't be silent. Give way to your grief and rail against its cause. Unless you express your grief, it will eat at you from inside and break your overburdened heart."

Despite having already been told the answer, Macduff asked, "My children, too?"

"Wife, children, servants, all who could be found in the castle and on your land," Ross said.

"And I was not there because I was seeking Malcolm," Macduff said. "Macbeth killed my wife, too?"

"Yes," Ross said. "I have told you that."

"Be comforted," Malcolm said. "Let revenge against Macbeth be your medicine to cure this deadly grief."

Such words were not comforting to Macduff, who said to Ross about Malcolm, "He has no children."

Macduff added, "All my pretty ones are dead? Did you say all? Hell! All? What, all my pretty chickens and their dam killed at one fell swoop?"

Malcolm said, "Fight it like a man."

"I shall do so," Macduff said, "but I must also feel it like a man. I cannot help remembering that of all people these were the most precious to me. Did Heaven witness their murders and would not help them? Sinful Macduff, Macbeth killed them because of you! They had done nothing wrong. Macbeth killed them because I came to England. Heaven rest them now!"

"Let this be the whetstone of your sword," Malcolm said, "Let grief convert to anger. Do not blunt your heart; instead, enrage it."

"I could act like a woman and cry," Macduff said. "I could also brag about how I will avenge their deaths. But I pray that Heaven will not make me wait but instead quickly bring me face to face with this fiend of Scotland. If I get within sword's length of him and he does not die — but he will die! — then let Heaven forgive him."

"Now you are speaking like a man," Malcolm said. "Let us go to Edward the Confessor. Our army is ready, and everything is ready for us to march against Macbeth, who is soon to fall from power. God will show us our way. Macbeth has made a long night for Scotland, but we will make it day."

CHAPTER 5: THE FALL OF MACBETH

— 5.1 —

In an anteroom in Macbeth's castle at Dunsinane, a doctor and a gentlewoman — a woman of high social standing — talked together.

The doctor said, "I have for two nights stayed up and watched with you, but I have seen nothing of what you have reported to me. When was it Lady Macbeth last sleepwalked?"

The gentlewoman replied, "Ever since Macbeth took his soldiers out to try to stop the rebellion of the nobles, I have often seen her rise from her bed, throw her nightgown upon her body, unlock her chest, take out paper, fold it, write upon it, read it, afterwards seal it, and again return to bed. She has done all these things despite being in a deep sleep."

"This is a great perturbation in nature, to receive the benefit of sleep and yet at the same time to do many things that are normally done while awake. Have you ever heard her say anything while she is sleepwalking?"

"Yes, sir, I have heard her say things that I will not repeat to you."

"You may tell me," the doctor said. "It is the right thing for you to do."

"I will not tell you or anyone else — not until I have a witness to confirm what I would say," the gentlewoman said.

Holding a candle, Lady Macbeth, sleepwalking, entered the room.

The gentlewoman said, "Look! Here she comes! This is what she often does. She is asleep — watch her, but stay hidden."

"Where did she get the candle?"

"It was by her bed. She always has candles lit by her at night. She has ordered that this be done."

"Her eyes are open," the doctor said.

"Yes, but she does not see anything. She is still asleep."

"What is she doing now?" the doctor asked. "Look how she rubs her hands."

"Seeming to wash her hands is a habit of hers. I have seen her do this for a quarter of an hour."

Lady Macbeth, thinking she saw King Duncan's blood on her hands, said, "Yet here's a spot."

59

The doctor said, "I will write down what she says. It will help me to remember her words."

Reliving the night that her husband and she murdered King Duncan, the sleepwalking Lady Macbeth said, "Out, damned spot! Out, I say!"

Reliving hearing the bell strike two the night of King Duncan's murder, Lady Macbeth said, "One. Two. Why, then, it is time to do it. Hell is murky! My husband, are you a soldier and afraid? What need we fear who knows what we will have done, when none will have the power to bring us to justice?"

Reliving when she smeared King Duncan's blood on the faces of his bodyguards, Lady Macbeth said, "Yet who would have thought the old man to have had so much blood in him."

"Did you hear that?" the doctor said.

Remembering the murder of Lady Macduff, Lady Macbeth said, "The Thane of Fife had a wife — where is she now?"

Reliving trying to wash her hands after she had smeared King Duncan's blood on the faces of his bodyguards, Lady Macbeth said, "What, will these hands never be clean?"

Reliving the banquet at which her husband had been startled when he thought he saw Banquo's ghost, Lady Macbeth said, "No more of that, my lord, no more of that — you will mar all unless you can appear to be innocent."

"For shame," the doctor said. "You have known what you should not."

"She has spoken something that she should not, I am sure of that," the gentlewoman said. "Heaven knows what she has known."

Lady Macbeth said, "Here's the smell of the blood still! All the perfumes of Arabia will not take away the smell of this blood!"

She sighed heavily.

"What a sigh she made!" the doctor said, "Her heart is gravely burdened."

The gentlewoman said, "I would not have such a heart in my bosom even if I were Queen."

The doctor said, "Well, well, well."

"Pray God all be well, sir," the gentlewoman said.

"This disease is beyond my medical knowledge, yet I have known some people who have walked in their sleep who have died holily and without guilt in their beds."

Lady Macbeth said, "Wash your hands, put on your nightgown, don't look so pale. … I tell you yet again, Banquo is buried — he cannot come out of his grave."

"This is something new," the doctor said.

Lady Macbeth said, "To bed, to bed! There is knocking at the gate. Come, come, come, come, give me your hand. What's done cannot be undone. To bed, to bed, to bed!"

Still asleep, Lady Macbeth walked out of the room.

"Will she go now to bed?" the doctor asked.

"Yes. Immediately," the gentlewoman said.

"Foul whisperings and evil rumors are abroad," the doctor said. "Unnatural deeds do breed unnatural troubles such as sleepwalking and sleeptalking — guilty minds will tell their secrets to their deaf pillows. Lady Macbeth needs a priest more than she needs a physician. May God forgive us all!"

He ordered the gentlewoman, "Look after her. Take away from her anything she can use to hurt herself. Watch her carefully."

He added, "Now, good night. She has baffled my mind and amazed my sight. I dare not tell anyone what I think."

"Good night, good doctor," the gentlewoman said.

— 5.2 —

The Scottish nobles Menteith, Caithness, Angus, and Lennox, as well as many Scottish soldiers, were in a field. These nobles — rebels against Macbeth — were planning to meet and join the soldiers led by Malcolm.

Menteith said, "The English army is near, led on by Malcolm, his uncle Old Siward and the good Macduff. They burn to get revenge against Macbeth. The causes they have for revenge would rouse even a dead man to the bloody and fierce call to arms against Macbeth."

Angus said, "We will meet the English army near Birnam Forest. That is the way their soldiers are marching."

Caithness asked, "Is Donalbain with his brother, Malcolm?"

"No, sir, he is not," Lennox replied. "I have a list of the gentry who are with Malcolm. Old Siward's son is with Malcolm, as are many beardless youths who are now declaring themselves to be men by marching against Macbeth."

"What is the tyrant Macbeth doing?" Menteith asked.

"He is fortifying his castle at Dunsinane," Caithness replied. "Some people say that he is insane. Other people, who hate him less, call it valiant fury. Either way, he lacks self-control, and he cannot control the soldiers who should be fighting for him. Because he lacks soldiers who are willing to fight for him in open battle, he is preparing for a siege."

"Now he can no longer blame his murders on other people, the way he blamed King Duncan's murder on the King's bodyguards and the King's sons," Angus said. "The blood of the people he has murdered now sticks to his hands. His subjects now continually rebel against him because of his many treacheries. He forces his soldiers to obey his orders — none of his soldiers obeys him out of respect. His crown is too large for him — he is not man enough to be King. His wearing the crown is like a dwarfish thief trying to wear a giant's robe."

"Everything that is inside Macbeth condemns his murders and other evils," Menteith said. "No wonder Macbeth's tormented senses and awareness of guilt cause him to recoil and startle and act in fits of irrational anger."

"Let us march forward," Caithness said. "We will obey the orders of Malcolm, the true King to whom we truly owe allegiance. He will be the doctor of our sickly country, and with our blood we will help him purge the evil that is Macbeth."

"We will use our blood to water the flower that is our rightful King and make it grow, and we will use our blood to drown the weed that is Macbeth," Lennox said. "Now let us march to Birnam Forest."

— 5.3 —

In a room in the castle at Dunsinane, Macbeth raged — the doctor and some servants witnessed his rage.

"Bring me no more reports," Macbeth ordered. "I know that the Thanes are deserting me and going to support Malcolm, and I don't care. Until Birnam Forest marches to Dunsinane, I shall fear nothing. What is the boy Malcolm to me? A danger? No! He was born of woman. Supernatural spirits that know the future of mortals have told me, 'Fear not, Macbeth; no man who is born of woman shall ever have power over you.' So desert me, disloyal Thanes, and support the effeminate and decadent English. My mind and my heart shall never sag with doubt nor shake with fear."

A servant, pale with fear, entered the room.

Macbeth yelled at the servant, "May Satan turn you black, you cream-faced fool! Where did you get that foolish look of fear? You look like a frightened goose."

His voice shaking with fear, the servant said, "There is ten thousand —"

Macbeth finished the sentence for him, "Geese, fool?"

"Soldiers, sir," the servant said.

"Go prick your face and use the red blood to cover the whiteness of your frightened face, you lily-livered boy! What soldiers, fool? May your soul die! Your linen cheeks are witnesses of your fear. What soldiers, milk-face?"

"The English force, so please you."

"Take your face away from here," Macbeth ordered.

The servant left the room.

Macbeth began to call for an officer, whose name was Seyton.

"Seyton!" Macbeth called. "I am sick at heart, when I see such cowards. Seyton, come here!"

Macbeth thought, *This battle will either establish me permanently on the throne or take the throne away from me.*

He paused, then he thought, *I have lived long enough. My life is now like a withered, dry, yellow leaf of autumn, ready to fall and die as winter arrives. All those things that an old man who has lived well should have — honor, love, loyalty, and troops of friends — I will not have. Instead, I will have curses that are not loud but are deep, the signs of honor that I force my subjects to show to me, and flattery — flattery that my subjects will not like to engage in but will be too afraid not to.*

He yelled, "Seyton!"

Seyton entered the room and said, "What is your gracious pleasure?"

"Is there any more news?"

"All that was reported to you has been confirmed to be true."

"I'll fight until my flesh is hacked from my bones," Macbeth said, "Give me my armor."

"It is not needed yet," Seyton said.

"I'll put it on anyway," Macbeth said. "Send out more people on horseback; let them scout the country around the castle and hang anyone who talks of fear. Give me my armor."

Then Macbeth said, "How is your patient, doctor?"

"She is not so sick, lord," the doctor said, "as she is troubled with numerous illusions and hallucinations that keep her from sleeping."

"Cure her of that," Macbeth ordered, "if you can. Can you treat a diseased mind? Can you remove her sorrows from her memory? Can you give her a drug that will clean away everything that weighs upon her heart?"

"Only the patient can heal that kind of illness," the doctor said.

"In that case, let medical science go to the dogs," Macbeth thundered. "I don't want it."

He said to Seyton, "Come, put my armor on. Give me my lance."

He said to the doctor, "The Thanes fly from me."

He said to Seyton, "Faster."

He said to the doctor, "If you are able to, analyze the urine of my country, discover what disease it suffers from, and cure it so that Scotland has a sound and pristine health. If you can do that, I will applaud you until the echo of my applause returns to you."

Having finished putting on his armor, Macbeth said to Seyton, "Pull my armor off, I say."

Macbeth said to the doctor, "What rhubarb, senna, or purgative drug would purge Scotland of these English soldiers? Have you heard about the soldiers?"

"Yes, my good lord," the doctor said. "I know that you are preparing for war."

Macbeth said to Seyton, who was holding the armor he had taken off Macbeth, "Carry the armor behind me. I will not be afraid of death and destruction and bane until Birnam Forest comes to Dunsinane."

Macbeth and Seyton left, and the doctor thought, *Were I from Dunsinane away and clear, a large sum of money would not again draw me here.*

— 5.4 —

Malcolm, Old Siward and Young Siward, Macduff, Menteith, Caithness, Angus, Lennox, and Ross rode horses near Birnam Forest. Many soldiers marched near them.

"Kinsmen," Malcolm said, "I hope the time is near at hand when Scots can again be safe in their own homes."

Menteith said, "All of us believe that will happen soon."

Old Siward asked, "What forest is this ahead of us?"

"Birnam Forest," Menteith said.

Malcolm ordered the soldiers, "Let every soldier cut down a branch and carry it in front of him. That way, we can hide the number of soldiers in our army and Macbeth's scouts will make false reports of our army's strength."

The soldiers replied, "We shall do it."

Old Siward said, "According to our own scouts, the impudent Macbeth is fortifying Dunsinane and will not attack us in open battle. He is willing to endure our setting siege to the castle."

"Dunsinane is his main fortress," Malcolm said. "He is forced to stay there. Whoever is able to desert him does so, whether they are nobility or common people. The soldiers who stay with him are forced to stay. They do not respect Macbeth and do not want to die for him. If Macbeth were to take the field, his soldiers would desert him."

Macduff said, "Let us do our judging of soldiers after the battle is over. For now, let us fight."

Old Siward said, "Soon we will find out whether we win or lose the war. We can talk and we can hope, but it will be fighting that wins the war."

— 5.5 —

In a room in the castle at Dunsinane stood Macbeth, Seyton, and some soldiers.

Macbeth ordered, "Hang our banners on the walls of the castle that face the enemy. The news is still, 'They come!' But the strength of our castle will laugh a siege to scorn. Let the enemy soldiers lay siege until famine and fever eat them up. If they were not reinforced with deserters from my army, we might have boldly met them in open battle, beard to beard, and beat them back to England."

Some women in the castle screamed.

"What is that noise?" Macbeth asked.

"It is the cry of women, my good lord," Seyton said. He left to investigate the cause of the screams.

I have almost forgotten what fear tastes like, Macbeth thought. *At one time, my senses would have cooled if I had heard a scream at night and my hair would have risen and stood on end when I heard a scary story. But I have experienced so many murderous horrors that they are so familiar to me that a new horror cannot startle me.*

Seyton entered the room.

"What is the cause of that screaming?" Macbeth asked.

"The Queen, my lord, is dead," Seyton replied.

"She should have died at a later time," Macbeth said. "Then I would have had time to mourn her. But she would inevitably die sometime, so now is as good a time as any."

He thought, *Tomorrow, and tomorrow, and tomorrow creep along from day to day until the end of time. And all our yesterdays have lighted fools the way to dusty death. Out, out, brief candle of life! Life is only a walking shadow that passes quickly away. Life is only a poor actor who struts and frets his hour upon the stage and then is heard no more. Life is meaningless: It is a tale told by an idiot, it is full of sound and fury, and it means nothing.*

A messenger entered the room.

"You came here to tell me something," Macbeth said. "Tell me quickly what you have to say."

"My gracious lord," the messenger said, "I need to report to you what I saw, but I do not know how to do it."

"Just tell me," Macbeth ordered.

"As I was doing guard duty on the hill, I looked toward Birnam Forest, and it seemed to me that the forest began to move."

"Liar and slave!" Macbeth raged.

"If I am lying, punish me," the messenger said. "Look for yourself and you will see the forest is now only three miles away and moving toward us."

Macbeth said, "If you are lying, I will hang you alive from the nearest tree and let you die of hunger. If you are telling the truth, I will not mind if you do that to me."

Macbeth thought, *My confidence is disappearing, and I suspect that the apparition the three Weird Sisters showed me was equivocating and deliberately misleading me, making me think that one thing is true when actually something different is true. The apparition told me, "Fear not, until Birnam Forest comes to Dunsinane."*

Macbeth said, "Let us not wait to be besieged! Instead, let us arm for battle and go forth from the castle! If this messenger is telling the truth, it is no use for me either to try to run away or to stay here and endure a siege."

Macbeth thought, *I begin to grow weary of the Sun and of life itself. I wish that the universe were plunged into chaos.*

Macbeth said, "Ring the alarm bell! Blow, storm! Come, vengeance!"

Macbeth thought, *At least I'll die with armor on my back.*

He had decided that if he should die, so be it. Still, he had some confidence in the third apparition's prophecy: "No man born of woman shall harm Macbeth."

— 5.6 —

Malcolm, Old Siward, and Macduff, along with many soldiers holding tree branches in front of them, stood outside Macbeth's castle at Dunsinane.

Malcolm ordered, "We are close enough to the castle. Throw down the leafy tree branches and show yourselves to the enemy. Old Siward, you and your noble son, Young Siward, shall lead our first battalion. Macduff and I will do whatever else is needed to be done."

Old Siward replied, "Fare you well. We go to find the tyrant's army. If we cannot conquer the tyrant, we deserve to be beaten."

"Make all our trumpets speak," Malcolm said. "Blow all of them. Give them all breath, those noisy announcers of blood and death."

— 5.7 —

Macbeth had led his few forces out of the castle and onto the battlefield, where they were badly losing.

Macbeth thought, *I am like a bear that is tied to a stake for the night's bloody entertainment of a bear fighting dogs. I cannot run away, but I must fight the dogs that attack me. Who is the man, if anyone, who was not born of woman? I must fear that man, or no man.*

Young Siward saw Macbeth and asked him, "What is your name?"

"If I tell you my name, I will frighten you," Macbeth said.

"No, you won't," Young Siward said. "Not even if you have a name that is hotter than any name in Hell."

"My name is Macbeth."

"Satan himself could not pronounce a name that is more hateful to my ear."

"Or one that makes you more afraid."

"You lie, hated tyrant! With my sword I will show you that your name causes no fear in me!"

Macbeth and Young Siward fought, and Macbeth killed Young Siward.

Macbeth said over the corpse, "You were born of woman, but I smile at the swords and laugh at the other weapons of all men who were born of woman."

Macduff, who was seeking Macbeth elsewhere on the battlefield, shouted, "I seek the place where the most fighting is because that is where Macbeth will be. Tyrant, show your face! If you are already slain by no stroke of mine, my wife's and my children's ghosts will continue to haunt me. I will not strike at wretched foot soldiers, mercenaries who bear arms for money. Either I kill you, Macbeth, or I sheathe my sword with an unbloodied and unbattered edge. The great clamor I hear must be announcing your presence. Let me find Macbeth, god of Fortune! I ask for nothing more."

Elsewhere, Old Siward and Malcolm met and talked about the battle.

"This way, my lord," Old Siward said to Malcolm. "The castle surrendered to us without a fight. Most of the tyrant's soldiers have turned against him and are now on our side. The battle is almost won. Little is left to do."

Malcolm said, "We have met with 'enemy' soldiers who join our cause and fight by our sides against a common enemy: Macbeth."

"Sir, enter the castle," Old Siward said.

5.8

Macbeth, knowing that he had lost the battle, thought, *Why should I play the Roman fool, and commit suicide by throwing myself on my own sword? Let Brutus or Cassius commit suicide when they see that their cause is lost. While I see enemy soldiers, gashes made by my sword look better on their bodies.*

Macduff saw Macbeth and ordered, "Turn around, Hell-hound, turn around!"

Recognizing Macduff, Macbeth said, "Of all men, I have been avoiding you. Don't fight me. My soul is already too much burdened with the blood of your wife and children. I do not want to add your blood to my burden of guilt."

"I will not talk," Macduff said. "My sword will do the talking. You are a bloodier villain than words can express."

Macduff attacked Macbeth, who fiercely fought back.

At a pause in the fight, Macbeth said to Macduff, "You are wasting your time trying to kill me. You can kill air with your sword as easily as you can kill me. Go and fight soldiers who can be killed. I lead a charmed life. No man born of woman can kill me."

"Your charm is worthless," Macduff replied. "The evil spirit whom you have served and still serve can tell you that I was from my mother's womb prematurely ripped. I was not born through the birth canal but had to be cut out of her womb to save my life."

"May you be damned to Hell for telling me this!" Macbeth shouted. "You have taken away my confidence. Let no one believe the Weird Sisters — those deceiving fiends who trick mortals with equivocating words that appear as if they are good but that are in reality evil. I will not fight you."

"Then surrender, coward," Macduff said. "We will exhibit you before the gaze of your former subjects. We will treat you the way we treat deformed animals and make you a freakshow. We will paint your portrait on a sign on a pole along with the words 'Here may you see the tyrant'!"

"I will not surrender and kiss the ground before young Malcolm's feet, and I will not be subjected to cruel treatment and abuse by my subjects," Macbeth said. "Although Birnam Forest has marched to Dunsinane and although you are not of woman born, yet I will try to kill you. In front of my body, I hold my shield. Fight, Macduff, and damned be the first man who cries, 'Stop! I have had enough!'"

They fought.

Elsewhere, Malcolm, Siward, Ross, and the other Thanes were meeting.

"Not all of our friends are accounted for," Malcolm said. "I hope that they survived the battle."

"Some soldiers die in every battle," Old Siward said. "Judging by the number of corpses we see, we have won a great battle while losing very few lives."

"Macduff is missing, and so is your noble son," Malcolm said.

Ross said to Old Siward, "Your son, my lord, has paid a soldier's debt on the battlefield. He lived only until he reached adulthood. As soon as he became an adult, he proved his manhood by valiantly fighting. He died courageously, as befits a man."

"My son is dead?" Old Siward asked.

"Yes," Ross replied. "His corpse has been carried off the battlefield. If you were to mourn him as much as he is worth, you would never stop mourning him."

"Were his wounds in the front?" Old Siward asked, knowing that cowards who run away are wounded in the back.

"Yes, they were in the front," Ross replied.

"Then he deserves to be — and is — a soldier of God," Old Siward said. "Had I as many sons as I have hairs, none could have a more honorable death than that of Young Siward. And so the death bell tolls for my son."

"He deserves to be mourned more greatly than this," Malcolm said, "and I shall mourn him."

"No greater mourning is needed," said the stoical Old Siward. "He died well and honorably. He settled all of his accounts. Look! Here comes better news!"

Macduff, carrying the decapitated head of Macbeth, said to Malcolm, "You are now King. Hail, King! Look at the cursed head of the tyrant. Scotland is now free from tyranny. I see around you the nobles of Scotland, and I ask them to join me in this cry: Hail, King of Scotland!"

Macduff and the nobles shouted, "Hail, King of Scotland!"

Malcolm said, "Not much time will pass before I reward you for your loyalty. I owe you now, and I will repay you. My Thanes and kinsmen, henceforth be Earls — the first Earls ever in Scotland. Much remains to be done with the dawn of this new era. We must call from abroad our friends in exile who fled from Macbeth's tyranny. We must find the cruel supporters of this dead butcher and his fiend-like Queen, who is thought to have committed suicide. These and other things, God willing, we will do justly and at the right time and place. Thank you, all, and I invite you to see me crowned at Scone as the rightful King of Scotland."

APPENDIX A: ABOUT THE AUTHOR

It was a dark and stormy night. Suddenly a cry rang out, and on a hot summer night in 1954, Josephine, wife of Carl Bruce, gave birth to a boy — me. Unfortunately, this young married couple allowed Reuben Saturday, Josephine's brother, to name their first-born. Reuben, aka "The Joker," decided that Bruce was a nice name, so he decided to name me Bruce Bruce. I have gone by my middle name — David — ever since.

Being named Bruce David Bruce hasn't been all bad. Bank tellers remember me very quickly, so I don't often have to show an ID. It can be fun in charades, also. When I was a counselor as a teenager at Camp Echoing Hills in Warsaw, Ohio, a fellow counselor gave the signs for "sounds like" and "two words," then she pointed to a bruise on her leg twice. Bruise Bruise? Oh yeah, Bruce Bruce is the answer!

Uncle Reuben, by the way, gave me a haircut when I was in kindergarten. He cut my hair short and shaved a small bald spot on the back of my head. My mother wouldn't let me go to school until the bald spot grew out again.

Of all my brothers and sisters (six in all), I am the only transplant to Athens, Ohio. I was born in Newark, Ohio, and have lived all around Southeastern Ohio. However, I moved to Athens to go to Ohio University and have never left.

At Ohio U, I never could make up my mind whether to major in English or Philosophy, so I got a bachelor's degree with a double major in both areas, then I added a Master of Arts degree in English and a Master of Arts degree in Philosophy. Yes, I have my MAMA degree.

Currently, and for a long time to come (I eat fruits and veggies), I am spending my retirement writing books such as *Nadia Comaneci: Perfect 10*, *The Funniest People in Dance*, *Homer's* Iliad: *A Retelling in Prose,* and *William Shakespeare's* Othello: *A Retelling in Prose.*

By the way, my sister Brenda Kennedy writes romances such as *A New Beginning* and *Shattered Dreams.*

APPENDIX B: SOME BOOKS BY DAVID BRUCE

Retellings of a Classic Work of Literature

Arden of Faversham*: A Retelling*

Ben Jonson's The Alchemist: *A Retelling*

Ben Jonson's The Arraignment, or Poetaster: *A Retelling*

Ben Jonson's Bartholomew Fair: *A Retelling*

Ben Jonson's The Case is Altered: *A Retelling*

Ben Jonson's Catiline's Conspiracy: *A Retelling*

Ben Jonson's The Devil is an Ass: *A Retelling*

Ben Jonson's Epicene: *A Retelling*

Ben Jonson's Every Man in His Humor: *A Retelling*

Ben Jonson's Every Man Out of His Humor: *A Retelling*

Ben Jonson's The Fountain of Self-Love, or Cynthia's Revels: *A Retelling*

Ben Jonson's The Magnetic Lady, or Humors Reconciled: *A Retelling*

Ben Jonson's The New Inn, or The Light Heart: *A Retelling*

Ben Jonson's Sejanus' Fall: *A Retelling*

Ben Jonson's The Staple of News: *A Retelling*

Ben Jonson's A Tale of a Tub: *A Retelling*

Ben Jonson's Volpone, or the Fox: *A Retelling*

Christopher Marlowe's Complete Plays: Retellings

Christopher Marlowe's Dido, Queen of Carthage: *A Retelling*

Christopher Marlowe's Doctor Faustus: *Retellings of the 1604 A-Text and of the 1616 B-Text*

Christopher Marlowe's Edward II: *A Retelling*

Christopher Marlowe's The Massacre at Paris: *A Retelling*

Christopher Marlowe's The Rich Jew of Malta: *A Retelling*

Christopher Marlowe's Tamburlaine, Parts 1 and 2: *Retellings*

Dante's Divine Comedy: *A Retelling in Prose*

Dante's Inferno: *A Retelling in Prose*

Dante's Purgatory: *A Retelling in Prose*

Dante's Paradise: *A Retelling in Prose*

The Famous Victories of Henry V: *A Retelling*

From the Iliad *to the* Odyssey: *A Retelling in Prose of Quintus of Smyrna's* Posthomerica

George Chapman, Ben Jonson, and John Marston's Eastward Ho! *A Retelling*

George Peele's The Arraignment of Paris: *A Retelling*

George Peele's The Battle of Alcazar: *A Retelling*

George Peele's David and Bathsheba, and the Tragedy of Absalom: *A Retelling*

George Peele's Edward I: *A Retelling*

George Peele's The Old Wives' Tale: *A Retelling*

"

William Shakespeare's 38 Plays: Retellings in Prose
William Shakespeare's 1 Henry IV, aka Henry IV, Part 1: *A Retelling in Prose*
William Shakespeare's 2 Henry IV, aka Henry IV, Part 2: *A Retelling in Prose*
William Shakespeare's 1 Henry VI, aka Henry VI, Part 1: *A Retelling in Prose*
William Shakespeare's 2 Henry VI, aka Henry VI, Part 2: *A Retelling in Prose*
William Shakespeare's 3 Henry VI, aka Henry VI, Part 3: *A Retelling in Prose*
William Shakespeare's All's Well that Ends Well: *A Retelling in Prose*
William Shakespeare's Antony and Cleopatra: *A Retelling in Prose*
William Shakespeare's As You Like It: *A Retelling in Prose*
William Shakespeare's The Comedy of Errors: *A Retelling in Prose*
William Shakespeare's Coriolanus: *A Retelling in Prose*
William Shakespeare's Cymbeline: *A Retelling in Prose*
William Shakespeare's Hamlet: *A Retelling in Prose*
William Shakespeare's Henry V: *A Retelling in Prose*
William Shakespeare's Henry VIII: *A Retelling in Prose*
William Shakespeare's Julius Caesar: *A Retelling in Prose*
William Shakespeare's King John: *A Retelling in Prose*
William Shakespeare's King Lear: *A Retelling in Prose*
William Shakespeare's Love's Labor's Lost: *A Retelling in Prose*
William Shakespeare's Macbeth: *A Retelling in Prose*
William Shakespeare's Measure for Measure: *A Retelling in Prose*
William Shakespeare's The Merchant of Venice: *A Retelling in Prose*
William Shakespeare's The Merry Wives of Windsor: *A Retelling in Prose*
William Shakespeare's A Midsummer Night's Dream: *A Retelling in Prose*
William Shakespeare's Much Ado About Nothing: *A Retelling in Prose*
William Shakespeare's Othello: *A Retelling in Prose*
William Shakespeare's Pericles, Prince of Tyre: *A Retelling in Prose*
William Shakespeare's Richard II: *A Retelling in Prose*
William Shakespeare's Richard III: *A Retelling in Prose*
William Shakespeare's Romeo and Juliet: *A Retelling in Prose*
William Shakespeare's The Taming of the Shrew: *A Retelling in Prose*
William Shakespeare's The Tempest: *A Retelling in Prose*
William Shakespeare's Timon of Athens: *A Retelling in Prose*
William Shakespeare's Titus Andronicus: *A Retelling in Prose*
William Shakespeare's Troilus and Cressida: *A Retelling in Prose*
William Shakespeare's Twelfth Night: *A Retelling in Prose*
William Shakespeare's The Two Gentlemen of Verona: *A Retelling in Prose*
William Shakespeare's The Two Noble Kinsmen: *A Retelling in Prose*
William Shakespeare's The Winter's Tale: *A Retelling in Prose*